MOMENTS
OF
MADNESS

To all my villain lovers out there, whose hearts flutter when they enter the scene...

Tell me baby, who hurt you?

COPYRIGHT @ T.L. SMITH 2023

MOMENTS OF MADNESS

by T.L. Smith

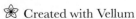 Created with Vellum

Warning

This book contains sexually explicit scenes and adult language and may be considered offensive to some readers. This book is intended for adults ONLY. Please store your books wisely, where they cannot be accessed by under-aged readers.

Blurb

We met at his ex's wedding, where she uttered their safe word in her vows. Immediately his jaw clenched, and his hands balled into tight fists. Then moments later, he told her I was with him. When in reality, I had snuck into the wedding. Knowing full well he was trouble, when I tried to leave, he gripped my arm and whispered in a low, intimidating voice.

"Do you sneak into weddings often?"

His words had me stuck to the spot.

It took only a few moments for me to realize this man was dangerous. The only logical thing I could do was kick him where it counts.

Little did I know that man was a hunter.

And it didn't take him long to find me…

ONE

Kyson

You are invited to the wedding of Lilly and Dale.
We ask that you dress in all white.
Please RSVP before the date noted below.

SWIFTLY, I crumple the card in my hand as I sit in my car, glaring at the venue where my ex is about to marry another man. I never thought it would bother me. I've been busy and being busy keeps my mind occupied. But right now I have the inclination to walk in and shoot up the place.

So why the fuck am I still sitting here?

Dress in white, it says.

Hmm, sure.

My head has been all types of fucked-up lately. And I can't seem to calm down. Gripping my leg hard to get it to stop it from bouncing, I look up. There are a few people I recognize, mostly members of *her* family. I'm not entirely sure why I decided to come, maybe to convince myself I don't need this; who would want this life she's chosen when they could have one like mine.

Somehow the lie doesn't sit right in my head.

My eyes scan the area outside; the wedding party's cars decorated with white bows, the moss-covered building, also flush with floral arrangements, and guests filtering in, all dressed in white. An odd choice in my opinion, but what do I know?

And who am I to judge, especially with what I do for a living. I tend to stick to black attire.

We didn't end on bad terms, Lilly and I, but nevertheless, we did end.

And that part was *all* me—absolutely *no* denying that fact.

Stepping out of the car, the man who has been patiently waiting so he can valet my car smiles as I hand him the keys.

Zuko, my older brother, told me not to attend.

I didn't tell Kenzo, my twin, as I didn't want to listen to the unrelenting backlash.

So here I stand, watching as guests file inside the venue. I stay until the last one is seen, and then I stand there a little longer than necessary.

The ceremony is about to begin, and I'm a little late.

Grinding my jaw, I turn back and think, *fuck it, I'm out*, but my car is gone, and I'm left standing there staring at the doors as the air conditioning from inside hits my back when the doors shut behind me. I haven't managed to make it all the way in, the doors just there waiting for me to go in, the white carpet under my black boots is nice, and I bet by the end of it, it will not be as white as it is now. Flowers are everywhere; red, white, and more white. Grinding my jaw, I stand there unsure what I should do.

Should I go in?

I shouldn't.

It seems everyone is inside waiting for the ceremony to begin, bar one, who doesn't look up as she approaches. She's small, tiny even. Her dress is too big for her, and yet she doesn't seem to care as it drags on the ground behind her. *Don't women usually lift their skirts when they walk?* I watch as she pulls a

3

small flask from between her tits, puts it to her mouth, and takes a swig.

Fuck, she has the right idea.

Now I wish I brought some hard stuff of my own.

The tiny thing stuffs the flask back between her tits just as quickly as she tore it out before she walks up the stairs and pulls open the massive door. Then she's inside and out of my view before I can blink—without even glancing at me once. Can't say that happens often; women like to stare as much as men do but they can be more subtle usually. Yet this one didn't even glance in my direction. Managing to walk in after her, I pull the very same door open and let it shut behind me. I spot a few of the bride's friends, the bridesmaids, straight away. One of them looks up, and I can't even recall her name, but I'm sure I've met her once. She scrunches her nose toward me as the doors open, the bridal party getting ready to start walking in.

"Sir, I must ask you to take your seat." Glancing to my left, I see a man standing there with a walkie-talkie in his hand. The bridesmaids begin walking as music starts to echo through the venue.

I hear the music immediately and pause.

Heels click on the stone floor, coming up behind me, and there she is…

Lilly.

Beautiful as always, wearing a white sleeveless dress with a lace skirt and a massive train. She spots me, pauses, and locks her emerald eyes on me. "Kyson."

I remember how she used to whisper my name from those plump, luscious lips.

"You aren't supposed to be standing there." As she says it, the man who ushered me in walks up and reaches for the door; it must have closed after the bridesmaids.

"You look beautiful," I tell her, because she does. Stunning. She is getting things from this man I would have *never* given her. It's why I ended things. Lilly deserves so much more.

"Sir, you need to move out of sight."

I step back as the doors are opened. Lilly's father is on the other side, and his eyes narrow at me, surely not expecting me to be here, before I smirk at him. Then they land on his daughter. Amicable or not, no father is going to be happy seeing the guy who broke his daughter's heart. And I did break her heart. Lilly loved me more than I could ever have loved her. It's just how some things

5

go. He offers his arm, and she takes it with one brief glance back at me.

Could I have changed for Lilly? Possibly.

She wanted me out of the life I am in.

Back then, I wasn't willing.

But lately, I've been thinking differently.

I'm not sure this is the life I want forever.

In fact, I've already told Zuko I want out.

I've earned enough money to never have to work again.

Contract murder pays well.

Extremely well.

I stand there for what feels like an eternity until the music stops. After stepping in through the open doors, I find the closest seat at the back and slide into it. I look up, and Lilly's smiling at her soon-to-be husband, and my leg starts bouncing.

Do I want this?

The white wedding.

A bunch of hypocrites smiling with false congratulations when they're either envious or there for God knows why, like me.

I want what Zuko and Alaska have, but let's be real, what are the chances of falling in love with a woman who's going to be content to be in a relationship with a contract killer, let alone marrying him?

Movement next to me has me turning to see the little bird, who obviously likes to drink, throwing back another swig from her flask.

Who is this woman?

"Care to share?" I ask her, nodding to her flask.

She pulls it away from her mouth and wipes her pink lips.

Fuck! They are some good cock-sucking lips, that's for sure.

"Fuck off." Her voice is sweet. So sweet I almost miss the words that actually came with it. She faces forward and slides the flask back down her dress top and looks at the happy couple exchanging vows.

"Dale, I take you, and only you, to be my husband. If I ever get feisty…"

That's all I hear.

I'm standing before I can stop myself, my hands fisted at my sides.

A few people turn back to see what the commotion is about, and Lilly looks back over her shoulder.

She fucking knows.

Of course, she fucking knows.

Dale, on the other hand, looks around with

7

confusion etched in his forehead. He has no idea what she just did.

She smirks before she spins back to Dale and continues her vows.

What a cunt.

"Yo, sit the fuck down so people stop staring this way." The little bird next to me pulls at my jacket, and I go willingly back to the seat.

"Give me some of your drink, or I'll reach between your tits and grab it myself."

"That's assault, dick." She reaches in, screws off the top, and I go to take it, but she puts it to her lips and chugs the last drop. When she pulls the flask away from her lips, she turns to me. "All gone. Now fuck off and find your own."

Goddammit! I look back to Lilly.

Her vows are finished, and Dale is now saying his.

How could she?

Who the fuck does she think she is using that word in her vows? Especially knowing there was a chance I would attend the ceremony.

"You're grunting. Stop it. People are looking."

Fuck, this bitch is annoying. I turn and notice her white dress is way big. I mean, I saw the length when she walked up the stairs, and it was dragging behind her, but damn, it swims on her.

"You couldn't find something that fits?" I grumble at her.

"You can't shut your fucking mouth long enough to have a sensible thought, can you?" she grumbles back.

Touché.

I hear that word again, and my eyes fly to the front of the room. Lilly only glances my way one more time, her eyes checking the room to try to hide the fact she is staring at me for my reaction, and before I know it, I'm standing and walking out.

She used *that word.*

A word that meant something to us.

Did she invite me to do this and rub it in?

What a bitch.

While walking, I check back over my shoulder and know the moment Lilly's eyes find mine because she smiles, then she beams at her now husband before he kisses her.

No one notices me leave.

I wonder if he knows he's kissing the mouth that just uttered *our* safe word.

She always was a cunning little minx.

But this is a *whole new level* of deviousness.

TWO

Kalilah
___

I SHOULDN'T BE HERE.

I should leave.

But…food. And I'm more than a little drunk.

What can I say? Weddings do that to me. Maybe it's all the organza and champagne-colored table clothes, crystal glasses, and shimmering silver-ware. Or the fake smiles of the guests who are offering their congratulations, but in their own lives, they are fucking the secretary or drinking gin at ten in the morning just to get through the day. It could also be something else I don't want to dwell on.

The waitress is weaving through the guests while holding a tray full of food, so I reach over and take more than a couple of shrimp canapes before I turn around. And that's when I spot him again. He's standing in front of the bride. The squeezed fists by his sides are at odds with the slightly disinterested, slightly polite expression on his face. I get the distinct impression he has a mouthful to say but is keeping quiet either for the bride's sake—there are a bunch of people standing around waiting to congratulate the bride—or because he's waiting for the right moment. Good or bad. Somehow, he doesn't strike me as the kind of guy who will take anyone's feelings into account.

I wonder who he is.

I have a feeling he's from the bride's side, but how exactly?

He was definitely upset when she read her vows, but then he left.

Do they have a history?

I start moving toward them. My head is tilted down when I reach them so I can listen to what they're saying. Lifting my hand to put some more food in my mouth, I'm almost run over by a hulking man.

"Fucking hell," I mutter as the food is smashed into the side of my mouth instead of going inside it.

"You have such a foul mouth for a lady." I raise my head to a man whose eyes are so dark they look almost completely black.

"Who said I was a lady?"

"Is this your date?" the bride asks him. *Shit.*

"You don't know her?" the stranger asks.

The bride gives me a once-over and narrows her eyes. "No, I don't." She pauses. "Who invited you?"

"I did," the stranger says, his gaze firmly fixed on me, as the bride's eyebrows squeeze together in confusion. *You and me both, girl.* He read me way too fast for my liking. But before the bride can utter another word, he turns back to her. "I know what you did, Lilly. Does your husband know you used our safe word in your wedding vows?"

If that food I'd eaten earlier landed in my mouth, I probably would have choked on it right then and there. The bride, also now known as Lilly, side-eyes me, her cheeks red, before she leans into him. "I didn't—"

He tsks at her, effectively cutting her off.

"You may be able to lie to him, but not me. You know better than that." Her hands start to fidget with the skirt of her dress, and I almost feel bad for her, but I have a feeling what he's saying is true and possibly the reason he stormed out of the ceremony.

Just as she goes to speak, her husband walks up and places his arm around her back, cuddling her.

She straightens, and the stranger smiles.

"Kyson, it's good to see you." The husband offers him his hand, and Kyson looks at it like it might burn him. The cogs are turning in his head—*should he or shouldn't he*—but then he reaches out and shakes it before he pulls back and slides his hand into his pocket.

"Congrats are in order, I guess," Kyson says.

"Yes, now if you would excuse me, I need to take my wife." The husband looks behind him at someone else, clearly wanting his wife away from Kyson. Not that I blame him. Kyson is very attractive. Cocky as well.

"Be careful with that one…" Kyson's jaw clenches. "She's feisty."

The bride pales at his words, and I stand there smiling as the newlyweds walk off with a single, worry-filled backward glance from the bride.

Then he says, "You." Kyson is in front of me. Way too close for comfort. "Do you sneak into weddings often?"

I go to turn away, but he catches my wrist, and I pale. He should *not* be touching me. Quickly, before I can even think, I lift my foot and kick out, landing a direct hit on my intended target—the spot between his legs. He drops my hand and cups his balls, and before I even worry about possible consequences, I'm hurrying out of there.

His eyes track me, but I don't care.

I need out.

I shouldn't have come.

But I was hungry.

And hunger makes you do silly shit.

"Miss…" one of the dreary-suited guys with a walkie-talkie calls out. I don't stop until I'm outside, where I kick these ridiculous shoes off and start running.

This is something I have experience with. I ran away from my hometown months ago, but I had money then. I swear I did. But when you can't find a job and don't want to give the government any personal information, you run and you hide, and now steal.

Is it really stealing, though? Especially if they have the means to replace it.

Because I don't—

Okay, yes, it is stealing. But I do try to justify it to myself, not that it works well, but I have figured out an easy way to get a full stomach.

And the best place to steal food? Weddings.

This is my third wedding this week, and I'm lucky I haven't gotten caught.

Until him.

I don't know him.

And I'm not sure I want to.

Kyson is a mystery and one that can fuck right off. I have enough shit happening in my life—I don't want nor need the worry of a man.

I manage to make it back to the shitty-ass motel I'm staying in and fall onto the bed. All the money I had left has gone into this place, which means I have no money for food. At the time, a place to stay seemed way more important than food.

I'm not sure I was right.

But I have this place for another few days, which gives me time to find another job. The problem is that it's incredibly difficult to find someone to hire you when you don't have references or a permanent address. I guess I could put this motel down, but then I leave a trace, and if *he* finds out where I am…

Well, let's just say I have to sleep with a knife under my pillow, and it's not just because of the neighborhood.

This neighborhood is not good—it's why the nightly rates are so cheap. Next door there is a strip club, and I've spoken to a few girls who work there as they came out for a cigarette break. I've dabbled with the idea of getting a job there.

The thing is, though, I'm not built like them.

I'm small in every way possible. My tits are barely big enough to need a bra, and my height gives the impression I'm younger than I am.

I asked one of the girls one night if they were hiring.

They laughed. And that was the end of that.

But if I have to shake my ass for strangers for a roof and food, I fucking will.

And that's a fact.

THREE

Kyson

_____

"YOU WENT," Zuko says as he slides on his boots. My older brother and I look alike, but my twin and I looked identical growing up . Then as we grew older, we grew apart in many ways, looks included. Both of us have gone to Zuko if we need anything. Or just to talk. Zuko knows how to listen. It's one of my favorite things about him. "Kyson," he says, shaking his head when I don't answer him.

"I was bored," I reply.

"Lies," he says, just as his girlfriend steps out of the bedroom, in only his shirt. "Avert your eyes before I pluck them out."

I smile and focus on Zuko.

"I'm your brother," I remind him.

"And she's _mine._"

"Hey, Kyson. Kill anyone today with your good looks?" Alaska teases, knowing full well it will make Zuko furious. She walks over and stands behind him before she wraps her arms around his neck.

"Oh, you know, it's daily. The ladies love me." Zuko gives me a death stare.

"Okay, well, I'm going back to bed. Toodles, lover," she says to Zuko and offers me a wave as she turns back for the bedroom.

"Stop staring at her ass." Zuko grunts.

"I wasn't. Is that my shirt she's wearing?" I point to where she left, and when Zuko raises his eyes to mine, I know I should stop. If I were anyone else, he would have used his knife on me by now.

"She said our safe word," I tell him, bringing him back to the wedding. "During her vows," I add.

His sour face drops, and he lifts his hand to brush his hair back before he shakes his head. "Well, fuck."

"Yeah, fuck."

"Okay, well, you can take the hit tonight. It will give you something to take out all that frustrated energy on. Don't say I never give you anything." He stands as the door opens, and Kenzo strolls in. Kenzo, I would say, is the more reserved of us, while Zuko is the ears and reason. And I am here to fuck shit up.

Zuko has knives, which he is an expert with.

Kenzo is the best sharpshooter I have ever seen. Plus, he can track almost anyone.

And me? Well, I…

Fuck if I know.

Let's be real—I just show up and take out the target.

"What's wrong?" Kenzo asks.

I say nothing as I step past him, but Zuko says, "He went to her wedding."

"Why didn't you tell me?" Kenzo asks.

I shrug as we walk out to make our way to the car. "You've been busy." In reality, I know that's not right, but I barely tell anyone anything. The one I talk to the most is Zuko because he knows I'm thinking of getting out.

Kenzo shakes his head. "I've been helping Grayson with the club. You know where I live. You could have come to me," he grumbles.

Grayson is probably the only other person we trust, apart from Pops, who gets us the hits. But now, we don't need Pops because our names alone are enough to attract attention. Those in our world know us, and they know us well.

Grayson runs a sex club that I'm sure Kenzo does more than help at. I've seen the cuts on him, so I'm sure he goes into the red room for some knife play. That place has many fantasy rooms for men, each is set up for their every need or want. And it's incredibly popular for "underground" men, who like to keep their shit secret. Grayson is good like that, and so is his woman, who helps him run the place.

"And you know where I live. I only see you at times like this," I add.

Kenzo stops as we get to the car.

Zuko pays us no attention as he slides in the driver's side and shuts the door.

"Is that the issue? Me not visiting you?" Kenzo asks.

"No," I tell him, swinging the door open and getting in.

"It sure as fuck sounds like it."

"When was the last time you saw me?" I ask as Zuko starts the engine and pulls out onto the road.

"Two months ago."

"Exactly." Shaking my head, I turn to Zuko. "When was the last time I saw you?"

"Last weekend," Zuko relays.

"So, what? You're mad that I don't visit?"

Kenzo asks. "Grow up!" There is no doubt that the mockery in his voice is evident.

"Fuck you, asshole."

"Sometimes, for someone so clever, you are dumb as shit," Kenzo says. "You know where I live as well. Fuckface."

"You never answer when anyone comes to your door," I remind him.

Zuko grunts next to me because he knows it's true. Kenzo hates having people in his space.

"What?" Kenzo huffs. "I don't like to let people in, but you two are different."

"I call bullshit," I say, shaking my head.

"Fuck you both."

Finished with this shit, I look out the window and see a mass of brown hair in a white dress holding a bottle of whiskey walking on the side of the street.

"Stop the car." I hit the dash, and Zuko pulls the car to the side of the road. I open the door and get out.

"What the fuck? We have a job," Kenzo shouts.

Glancing back into the car, I say, "You two do it. I'm out." Before they can argue, I run across the highway to where she can barely keep herself up straight. She's wearing the same white dress she wore at that wedding a few days ago, and she looks like a mess. Despite her size, she's easy to spot. The woman is a damn hellcat. It took days for my balls to recover from her blow.

While I walk over, her eyes are cast down, and the almost empty bottle of cheap as fuck whiskey sways precariously in her hand as she walks—or tries to walk. She grumbles something unintelligible and keeps on going. I sidestep and block her path again.

"Fucking hell, mister. Move," she slurs.

I want to chuckle at her words. They're so funny coming from something that looks so sweet she couldn't hurt a fly.

"Such nasty words for such a small bird," I tell her, and her head whips up, and her blurry, red eyes find mine.

"You," she seethes, lifting her bottle. She attempts to hit me with it, but I step to the side, and all it makes contact with is the air around her. She falls forward with the motion, and I grab the bottle from her. I watch, and as if in slow motion, she lands on her face.

Well, shit.

That probably hurt.

Sucks to be her.

But it could've been worse, I guess. She could have landed on the bottle.

"You good down there?"

She attempts to get up but then decides to just lie on the sidewalk. Arms at her sides as if she can't be bothered to even attempt to rectify her situation.

"You know someone has probably pissed where your face is, right?"

She says nothing, and when I lean down, I see that her eyes are closed. Poking her face with my finger, I get no response. I check her pulse as I hear footsteps approaching.

Looking up, I see both of my brothers standing there.

"Who's the chick?" Zuko asks, nodding to her.

"She kicked me in the balls at the wedding."

"So why did we stop?" Kenzo asks.

"Stop poking her," Zuko says, so I do it again for good measure. She turns her head to the other side. "She looks young," he notes.

"Her mouth says otherwise," I reply, remembering how she spoke to me. I reach for her wrist and turn it over. There's a butterfly tattooed on her skin and a small bag attached to her wrist. Removing the bag, I look inside, where there's an ID and nothing else. Not even a dollar.

Kenzo takes her ID card and studies it. "Twenty-three," he says, flicking the card back my way. "What do you plan to do with her?"

I stand and look down. "She can sleep here," I say, then turn to walk away.

"Kyson," Zuko says.

"What? She kicked me in the balls. She deserves it." A soft snore leaves her as I stride back. Reaching down, I lift her. She weighs almost nothing as I throw her over my shoulder. "Damn! This woman needs to eat something."

"She looks homeless," Kenzo adds.

"Fuck, we're late," Zuko says as we get to the car. "Put her in the back. We have to go." I do as he says and sit in the back with her, Kenzo taking the passenger seat. Glancing down at her head in my lap and her body tucked up into a small ball, I wonder why the fuck she's still wearing that dress. It's no longer white and has for sure seen better days. *What's her story?* Shaking my head, I look up to see Kenzo watching me.

"You went to see Lilly."

"I did."

"You left her," he adds like I need the reminder.

"I did," I reply.

His gaze flicks to the woman asleep next to me. I don't even know her name.

"She used their safe word in her vows," Zuko informs him and Kenzo's eyes go wide.

"Did you want to kill her?" Kenzo asks, obviously knowing me too well.

Because, you know, that's our answer to every damn thing.

We kill.

It's all we know.

And it works.

Incredibly fucking well.

"I thought about it."

"So why didn't you?"

"Because a part of me liked her. A lot."

"And she loved you," he adds, shaking his head. "Love is addicting. It's one of those things we should all steer clear of." He looks back to the snoring woman.

"I'm all in and don't plan to leave it," Zuko states, not an ounce of regret in his tone.

"Alaska is good for you," I say.

Zuko meets my eyes in the rearview mirror and nods. He knows I like Alaska for him. She's good for him and a little fucked-up, just like him. But good, nonetheless.

"Not us, brother," Kenzo says, referring to the two of us. "You tried love and failed. And now she married someone else."

His words hit me hard.

I wanted to love Lilly. I did. But for some reason, I couldn't. Not the type of love people talk about and not the type of love Lilly needed.

But then again, maybe I don't deserve that type of love.

FOUR

Kalilah

MY HEAD HURTS.

That's the first thing that comes to mind when I wake. The second thing I notice is that the floor isn't cold. When I drink too much, I always end up waking up on something cold. Managing to open one of my eyes, I see something black in front of me but it's blurry. My hands move, and I feel leather beneath my fingers.

Where am I?

I feel the effects of the alcohol in me. *Am I still drunk?*

Shit. I stole that bottle from a shop and ran. I was on the way back to my shitty motel, which I am about to lose soon.

And then I remember *him*.

What happened after I saw him?

Managing to sit up, I realize I'm in a car. *Whose fucking car am I in?* I reach for the door, but my arms are heavy and don't want to cooperate.

Stupid alcohol.

That's when I look out the window. And I wish I didn't. I wish I'd stayed asleep on the car seat and didn't sit up.

Because what is before me is not something I wish to see, or even hear, for that matter.

It's dark outside, but the car's headlights are trained on the man who sat next to me at the wedding. Kyson leans down and kisses the head of a man who is covered in blood before standing up and taking a step back. As he does, someone who looks like Kyson but different steps forward and raises a gun. He shoots. A scream rips from my mouth, and I scramble backward, but my back hits the door handle, causing me to hiss out a pained breath. Turning, I claw at the door, panic rising up my throat. *Shit! It won't open.* It has some sort of child lock, so I turn to try the other door, but when I glance back out the window, three sets of eyes are firmly fixated on me.

Quickly, I look away and climb through to the

front of the car. I manage to get the front door open with grabby hands, and then I fall out onto the ground. My hands hit the hard gravel, but I'm too panicked to react to the sting. Plus, I'm pretty sure I just ripped my dress.

Fuck.

"You look like a hot mess. Anyone told you that before?"

I know the sound of that voice. It's been stuck in the back of my head for some stupid reason. I grumble and shake my head as I attempt to get up. When I gaze up at Kyson, he is looking down at me with those dark, mesmerizing eyes. His arms are crossed over his chest, but then he offers me a hand to help me up. I try to focus on it, but I still feel pretty drunk. My head starts to spin, and he bends down to tuck his hand under my arm to help me up.

"I should have kicked you in the balls harder," I mumble. "Maybe then I wouldn't be here." He lets go of my arm, and I fall face-first into the ground. A small cry leaves my mouth, and I can taste my own blood.

"Maybe you need to rethink your situation. And watch how you speak to me."

The nerve of this asshole. Wiping at my mouth, two

29

other sets of boots stop in front of me. The owner of one of them leans down and helps me up.

I stand on wobbly legs.

Gosh, I shouldn't have drunk so much.

"Did you really just let her fall on her face?" the one holding me asks.

"Yes, she annoyed me," Kyson replies in an obvious tone. I hear a huff from the one holding me and turn to see he looks similar to Kyson, except his hair is a little longer, but the eyes are the same.

"Kyson," another voice says from behind me. I turn to see a third man standing next to Kyson. He looks mad, or maybe that's simply his normal facial expression. Glancing past the man in front of me to the man on the ground—the very same one Kyson kissed. He's lying in a pool of blood that is soaking the pavement.

Aside from the dim headlights, visibility is poor, and no one is around.

I start to scream. And as I do, Kyson steps up to me.

"Shut up, or I'll knock you the fuck out." He lifts his hand, and I scream. "Fucking hell," he mumbles as he covers my mouth. With his free hand, he lifts and removes me from the hold of the man who looks like him. He turns me so my back is pressed to his front. One of the men holds the car door open as Kyson pushes me in, his hand falling from my mouth as he does. I go to bite him, but he pulls back.

"Are you a rat?" he asks me.

"Fuck you. Let me go."

"To where? Where were you off to?" Kyson questions as the other two climb into the car, and we take off. "You look like shit…and smell like shit too." His nose crinkles up. "Do you have a shower?" I say nothing and scoot to the far end of the car, trying to climb out. It won't work, as I'm locked in here with three strange men.

"How long have I been with you?" I ask.

"You passed out maybe two or three hours ago," Kyson tells me. "You snore. It's annoying." He scrunches his nose again. I turn to the front and notice the one driving is not even paying me a lick of attention, but the other keeps glancing back at us.

"You live in a motel," the one in the passenger seat says. He glances down at something in front of him before he looks back at me. "Why?"

"Yeah, smelly…why?" Kyson taunts.

I lean over and hit Kyson, and he pulls away at my touch. At first, I feel rejected. This man, who is genuinely attractive, doesn't even want me to touch him, but then again, what do I care, right?

Fuck him.

I reach out again, only this time, I throw myself at him and manage to hit him on the cheek.

"Fuck, bitch! Slow down, you stink."

"Pull over," I yell. "Pull over!"

The driver does, and Kyson smirks.

"Where do you think you're going, little bird?"

"Away from you," I tell him.

"Kyson," the driver says, in a tone that has me worried. Kyson cracks his neck, his gaze locked on me.

"I know where you're staying, and I know who you are. You may not understand exactly who I am, but it's best you don't open your mouth about anything you heard or saw today."

"I'm going to let you live. And trust me when I say that's a privilege. But my brothers here…" he nods to the front, "will have no hesitation finding you, and whoever you love, and killing you if you talk. And believe me, the streets around here have ears, and they listen for us." I stay still and silent at his words. "Tell me you understand," he says, and I nod. "With your words," he orders.

"I-I don't want t-trouble. I hate the fact you even kn-know who I am," I stutter. "I keep a low profile for a reason."

I turn and reach for the handle and this time it's unlocked. As soon as I'm out of the car, I hurry away, not looking back. I make it to the edge of the river before I hear footsteps behind me. When I turn, Kyson is there. He holds out his hand, and I see the bottle I stole—it only has dregs left, but I take it anyway. I need something in my system to keep me warm once I'm kicked out of the motel and have no place to live.

"Go and shower. I bet your pussy stinks like rotten eggs."

What type of man even says that to a woman? I shake my head at him.

"You are such a pig. You know that?" I take a step back as he steps forward. He leans into me, and I can smell him. He smells fresh, clean, with something else I can't quite put my finger on.

"And you do stink," he whispers. He only pulls back slightly as his hand moves between us. He pushes me, and I miss a step on the ledge as I fall backward, landing in the water. The bottle drops from my hand, and I scream as I hear him chuckle.

"Someone needed to clean that pussy. Respect the pussy," he calls as he walks off.

I manage to climb out of the water, and when I look in the direction where the car was, he and his brothers are gone.

What a dick.

FIVE

Kyson
___

"CARE TO TELL us more about the girl and why she's still breathing?" Kenzo asks as we pull up to Zuko's.

We all remain in the car.

"Not particularly. I don't even know her name."

"Kalilah," Kenzo tells me. "It was on her ID, and after some searching, that is her real name, but she is currently using a fake last name." He pauses, waiting for me to speak. When I don't, he asks, "What's your fascination with her?"

"I don't have one."

Zuko huffs from the driver's seat and then gets out. Kenzo stays seated as Zuko walks off.

"You seem to be hiding a lot of stuff from me lately," Kenzo adds.

He's not wrong. I've been thinking of getting out of this life. But I love it. It's a double-edged sword. I'm not sure if I want to do this for the rest of my life, and that's my main issue. I know my brothers do because they were born to do this, but I feel more reserved about it.

Not that I'm not as good at the job as they are or anything like that.

It's more of…

It fucks up my life.

Out of the three of us, I always thought it would be me who would end up in a relationship, not Zuko. He's the coldest of us all, and yet there he is, hating spending time apart from Alaska and walking away from us without even a goodbye. The killing part I have no issues with, and to be frank I don't think I ever will. That's the part I struggle with the most. I'm good, and we are the best at what we do. But I also feel that it's not something I should be doing. If I want all the normal things in life, how could I chose to be a killer? It makes no sense—even in my brain.

"We aren't the same." And Kenzo knows it's the truth. While we may be twins, we have grown apart in more ways than one. We lived together for many years, and even then, somehow things just changed, so it was natural to get our own places. But I didn't realize with that also came less and less time when we would actually see each other. Not that I need to see my brother every day, but the only time lately I do see him is when we're on the job. And that's not the best time to talk. I think this is the most we've spoken to each other in months.

"You have your own life, and I have mine. You don't go out of your way to call or see me," I repeat what I said on the way to the hit.

"Neither do you."

"Lies," I tell him.

He huffs.

"In the beginning, I called you almost every week, but you hardly answered," I remind him.

He scratches his chin at my words.

I open the car door and slide out.

"I did some digging," he says, making me pause. "Seems your friend is broke. Dead broke. Not a cent to her name. My guess is that's why she was at the wedding and why she was drunk. She's either homeless or about to be if the motel hasn't kicked her out yet."

I look back over my shoulder at him.

"Maybe you should find out," he says.

Kenzo finally exits the car, and I watch as he

walks away, going to his motorcycle parked down the street.

Broke, that little bird is broke. How interesting. She fascinates me that one, not sure exactly why yet, maybe it's the back talk she throws at me, or the fact she looks at me with distain and a little bit of attraction rolled into one.

Maybe I'll pay Kalilah a visit.

Sitting in my car, I watch as she walks to her motel door. I've been here, waiting for her to return since I left my brothers.

Her dress is wet and filthy. She brushes her hair back from her face, and I wonder what it is about her that has stopped me from killing her. She's attractive, but she isn't the type I would usually go for. I like my women to have a bit of meat on them, and this woman looks like a starved animal, but she does have full lips that keep on popping into my head and a sweet, angelic voice that is as lethal as my kiss of death.

She bends down in front of her door and pulls a key card out from under the filthy doormat. Kalilah swipes it, and nothing happens. Then she stomps her foot on the ground as she tries again and again. A small scream leaves her lips as she throws her head back in frustration. I laugh at this. It amazes me she's still alive. How dumb can you be to leave a key card for your room under the mat, especially in this neighborhood?

She turns and strides to the front desk, her hands clutched at her sides. With more force than necessary, she pulls open the front door and storms through. I wonder what the person behind the desk thinks when they see her. *An angry little gremlin?*

That's what I see.

I can just make her out through the large windows of the lobby, her hands flying all about before she starts pointing at someone behind the counter. I step out of my car and lock it before making my way inside. I grab the handle just as I hear her scream. *What a dickhead he is.* I can't help the laughter that bubbles out of me just before I pull open the door. Neither of them look my way, too focused on their heated conversation about why the door won't open with her room card.

"You haven't paid," the man behind the counter says.

"Give me my things," she demands.

"You need to pay," the older dude says, crossing

his hands over his chest and sighing loudly at her. He is clearly becoming sick of her.

"How much?" I ask, and both heads whip toward me.

Her eyes narrow, and she flips me off. "Fuck off, you dick."

She has a few scrapes on her face, and I don't know if they're from when she fell on her face earlier or from another fall since. To be honest, they don't really make her face look any worse. They simply add a little bit of character.

"Fifty for the night," the dude yells at me, crossing his hands over his chest.

Fuck, she must be broke.

I pull out my card and place it on the counter. "Charge it for a month," I tell him, and his eyes light up.

"I'm not taking your money, you dick," she sneers, reaching for the card. But the guy behind the counter grabs it quickly and charges it anyway. "Give him his money and card back."

"Your room is unlocked. Next time, pay on time." He sits back down in his seat and holds the card up for me to take.

She huffs and stomps out, not even saying thank you.

Maybe I should teach her some manners.

Following her out, I find her opening her door and going inside. I manage to make it before the door shuts and put my foot between it and the door frame. Pushing it open, I see it's a small room that smells a bit rank. Scanning the tiny space, I quickly find her reaching for a bag of what appears to be clothes. She pulls out another dress, this one not quite as long as the one she has on, before she walks to what I am guessing is the bathroom.

"Do you have soap?" I ask her, scrunching up my nose.

"Will. You. Leave? I mean it. Get out." She swings around, hugging her dress to her chest as she glares at me.

"Why are you living here?" I ask as I walk to the bed. I look down to check what's in her bag. Well fuck! There are only a few items of clothing, and that's it. Is this all she is living with? How can this be good or healthy?

"Kyson, or whatever your name is… *Leave.*" She takes a few steps in my direction and waits. Just as she does, a few guys come to the door. Banging on it twice, they peek in.

"Oh, lookie what we have here. What a nice piece of ass you are." One of them licks his lips as he checks her out. The second steps inside, while the third stands outside the door, obviously in an attempt to keep guard.

And that's when I see the knife in his hand.

"We've been watching you. So young, so pretty." I doubt she's as young as they think. One of them turns to face me. "You should leave. It's our turn with her." I glance at Kalilah and see worry etched on her face, but she makes no move to ask me for help. Instead, she steps back.

"You must have the wrong room," I inform them.

Kalilah remains frozen where she is as they all step farther into the room.

The last one shuts the door behind him.

Big mistake.

"We don't make mistakes," the mouthy one spouts as he steps closer to me with his knife in hand.

I smirk at him. "What do you plan to do with that?" I ask, as my eyes glance toward the knife in his hand.

"Well, since you didn't take the advice and leave, it seems I'm gonna have to make you watch as I fuck that little piece of ass over there." He waves the knife at Kalilah, who gasps in shock and her eyes go wide before she attempts with shaky legs to step backward. One of the men steps closer to her, and she backs up. He reaches for her, and she kicks him in the dick. Hard. *Ouch.* I know that feeling well.

"Fucking bitch. Get her." The last one steps around his fallen friend, who is protecting his junk, as he makes his way to her. Kalilah kicks out again but misses as he sidesteps her and manages to grab hold. She fights him, and I watch her nails dig into his arm as her other hand tries to punch him in the face. The dress she was holding falls to the floor as she tries to get away from him. Her struggle is useless though. I see a glint of something at my side and step away, but the knife he was holding nicks my arm, slicing through my suit to cut my skin.

Fuck!

What a cock.

I turn to face him. He lunges for me again, and this time I manage to catch his wrist and flip him around. I bring the knife he's holding to his throat. He tries to let it go, but I manage to catch it and press it back against his skin. He screams and cusses at me, but I don't budge, and neither does he because he knows if he moves, the knife *will* cut him.

"Boys." The one that was fighting with Kalilah now has her in his arms.

She swears and keeps on trying to fight him off.

I like her.

Strong will, that one.

"Let him go," he says, gripping her to him.

"I just finished a job, dropped her into the lake, then my brothers go home. And I end up here, with you fools trying to what? Rape and murder her?" I ask them.

"Fuck off and leave. We just want the girl," the one in my arms says. The other one, who was on the floor, manages to stand. He locks eyes with me, and I tsk at him.

"Move any closer, and I'll cut his throat, then I will cut your balls off for good measure for not listening," I tell him.

"They will kill you...and her."

"I don't think I introduced myself to you all," I state, looking around the room. The guy holding Kalilah pauses but doesn't let her go as she kicks at him and looks to me.

"We couldn't care less who you are," the one I'm holding says.

"You should," I say, leaning into his ear. "I'm

Kyson." I smile, and he sees me from the corner of his eye. "Kyson Hunter."

I see when it registers with him. His mouth drops and his hands go straight into the air. Before he can speak another word, I kiss the top of his head, then smile before I slice his throat and step back so as not to get myself dirty.

"We're sorry." The one who was kicked in the balls wastes no time running, but I catch him before he can even get to the door. I slide the knife straight into his abdomen, and he drops to the floor. He goes to scream, but I pull the knife out and stab him right in his mouth.

I hear what appears to be vomiting, and when I turn around, I see Kalilah spewing all over the guy holding her with her eyes wide. He doesn't seem to care that his buddies are dead. He is more concerned with me walking toward him.

"Please, please," he begs. Pushing Kalilah toward me, I catch her and set her to the side. Just as he goes to pass me, I hold out my hand, and the knife pierces his cock. He screams and drops to the floor.

"I wouldn't do that if I were you," I tell her as I feel Kalilah start to move, and she pauses. "I can find you anywhere in the world, and you wouldn't like it if I had to hunt you down. Now close it," I say, referring to the door she's holding onto right now.

The guy on the floor is crying, and I reach for his neck and twist it. It pops loudly, and he drops to the floor.

I wipe my hands on my pants and turn back to her. "Now, where were we?"

SIX

Kalilah

CRAZY, insane. That's what he is.

It's like he goes through moments of madness. Watching him kill someone was truly horrifying and a work of art at the same time.

I've seen death before.

But to this extent? Never.

I shut the door because I believe his words. He would hunt me, and no matter how good I am at hiding, I have a feeling he will be able to find me.

Kyson pulls his cell from his pocket and presses a few buttons before he slides it back in. He steps over the dead body, coming toward me. "You still stink. Go shower. We can talk after." He glances down at the dress I dropped on the floor, and I reach down and pick it up.

Clutching it for dear life, I scurry off. "Leave the bathroom door open. Don't want you getting any ideas now, do we?" His voice is laced with annoyance.

I do as he says because I now know he has the ability to kill three men in just a few minutes. He could easily kill me without even breaking a sweat.

Stepping under the water, I pull the old, moldy curtain shut and turn the hot water on. It's a dismal trickle at best, but at least it works. Grabbing the only soap I have, which is a small bottle of shampoo, I wash myself and run it through my hair. I have no conditioner, which sucks, but it leaves my hair better than what it was—smelly and full of grime. Running my hands over my face makes it sting, but that's okay. I'm alive, and I'm not sure if I could say that if Kyson hadn't been here.

Reaching for the towel, I wrap it around myself as I get out. I then grab the dress I brought in and pull it over my head, carefully dropping the towel to the floor. My body is sore and in need of a worriless sleep. But I doubt I will get one of those for a long time.

My life is too crazy right now.

And here I thought running from my issues was a smart idea.

Maybe I was wrong.

"Come out, little bird," he calls from the room. When I do step out, I see two other men in the room, and not once do they look my way as they walk around. I notice then that two of the bodies are gone, and only one remains. "Clean-up crew," he answers my unasked question. "Now, pack your shit. You're coming with me." He nods to the door.

"I'm not going anywhere with you," I argue, crossing my arms over my chest.

Kyson steps closer to me, then even closer.

It's menacing.

It's madness.

"I'm not sure where I gave you an option there."

"You don't get that luxury," I tell him. "You don't own me."

"Ha! You either come with me or I put you down and let my men carry you out in one of those bags. Your choice." He smirks, knowing full well he has the advantage right now. And to be honest, do I really want to stay here?

I'm not sure.

Glancing at one of the men who's basically dressed in a hazard suit, I watch as he slides the body into a bag.

"Where will we go? You just paid for this room," I remind him. He brushes it off like it's nothing.

"You have two choices. Choose carefully because my patience is running thin right now." He cracks his neck from side to side before he continues. "One, you wait here, and my men take you." I look to the men who haven't even paid us a lick of attention. "Two, you come with me and stay at my place until I decide what to do with you. But under no circumstances are you to run. I want you to fully understand something…" He steps up closer and lifts a finger in front of my face. "No matter where you run, I *will* find you. I'll hunt you. No one can hide you from me." His words rock through me and I know he's telling the truth. Not only is he scary, I just saw what he can do.

He is dangerous. There's absolutely no doubt in my mind about that whatsoever.

"I'm a shit house guest," I inform him.

He grabs my bag, which has seen better days and starts toward the door.

"It's best you follow. If you don't, my men will take you."

I look around to see the men watching me.

Better the devil you know. For some reason, that's what pops into my head when it comes to him.

I follow him out to his car. It's nice. Black and fancy. He doesn't open my door, just gets straight into the driver's seat and throws my bag in the back like it's nothing. I glance around—it's dark and quiet. People are passed out on the streets, either from drugs or alcohol. It's an awful area, but it's all I could afford.

"Get in," he growls.

I do as he says and climb in. He takes off before I can even buckle myself in. This man has no care in the world for anyone. Not once does he say anything or look my way. It's as if I don't exist, yet I'm being forced to go to his house. He slows down as he reaches a set of closed gates. Pressing a button, they open to let him in.

I sit back and stare. Even though it's dark and there is only a porch light on, I can make out that this house is nice. I mean *real* nice. I grew up in a nice home. It was nothing fancy, but we were comfortable. My parents were good people, and possibly still are, but I can never go back. And I'm not sure I want to.

I'm such a disappointment.

They even told me so.

So I've been on my own for a while after I left he-who-shall-not-be-named. *Asshole.*

And I've been getting by, *barely.*

I want more for myself. I want to do more, earn my own way and live life.

But that's hard when no one wants to give you a chance.

Kyson stops the car, gets out, and grabs my bag from the back seat, not once asking me to follow as he walks to the front door. I know I have to get out, but I haven't moved. It's hard. Is he being nice, or does he plan to kill me?

Taking a deep breath, I step out of the car. After closing the door softly, my bare feet carry me along the cement driveway until I reach the large, black double doors which has one side open to allow entry into what seems like an open-planned living space. Stepping farther in, I see furniture that looks surprisingly homey as well as comfy. Wooden floors shine to an almost reflective finish, add to the flow of the room, and translate through to the dining area as well as the kitchen. I instantly smell clean, as in no mold or trash.

Is this how he lives? It must be nice.

Standing there for a good five minutes, I just stare. I can't say I'm accustomed to places like this, because I am not. Managing to finally move, I hear a noise and follow the sound to the kitchen, stopping when I see an older lady dressed in a nightgown making a coffee. She turns to me, a soft smile on her face as she holds a container of sugar in her hand. Her white hair is pulled back in a bun, and she has kind eyes.

"Hello, dear."

"Hi," I say, lifting a hand.

"Would you like a coffee? I made you some supper. It's on the table." She motions behind me, and when I turn, I see Kyson sitting at an ebony wood table and eating. He's concentrating on something on his phone and doesn't pay me a lick of attention. But the food, *wow.* The plate set in front of an empty leather chair is full—steak with veggies, biscuits, gravy, and a side salad. My mouth starts watering. "Hope it's okay, dear. Do you eat meat?"

I look back to the little old lady, wanting to cry, but manage to hold it in. "I do."

"Nancy, she will eat. Don't baby her," Kyson growls out. I take a deep breath and move to the table. I pull out the seat, but he still hasn't looked my way. Whatever's on his phone is interesting, that's for sure.

Picking up the knife and fork, I don't bother waiting for him to reply. I take in the art on the wall next to me as I stuff my face, literally. I'm surprised he has anything decorating his walls, least of all the colorful abstract art in purples and turquoise. When I look back at my plate, I'm pleased that I've only gotten through half the steak and veggies. I get the feeling I'm being stared at and look up to see his eyes are now on me. I wipe my mouth with the back of my hand and slow my chewing.

"How long has it been since you had a decent meal? Do you have no manners?" he asks softly, but it's filled with venom.

Chewing the last of what's in my mouth, I swallow, then answer, "None of your goddamn business, asshole." I stab another piece of steak, and the lady, Nancy, coughs from behind me as she brings over a glass of lemonade and places it in front of me.

She taps my shoulder to gain my attention. "I'll have breakfast ready in the morning. Do you have any requests?"

"Pancakes?" I ask, smiling. If he's going to force me to stay here, I'm going to take advantage. She nods and walks off, leaving me alone with Kyson. I look back at him and find him studying me.

"Do you have any form of manners?" he asks.

I fork up another piece of steak and put it in my mouth, not answering him. I stare at him as I chew. His jaw tics, and then I open my mouth and chew loudly. Now his jaw clenches hard as he stands and stomps off with his plate. I hear him throw it in the sink before he returns to the table—it's a wonder it didn't break—as I feel him come up behind me.

"Get up and follow me," he growls.

I place my fork down and slowly, painfully slowly, take a sip of my lemonade before I wipe my mouth with the back of my hand.

I feel full and fuck, it feels good.

Standing, I push my seat out and turn to face him. "Lead the way, boss." I smirk at him.

Kyson goes to speak, but then I guess he thinks better of it and turns to head out of the kitchen. I sigh and go after him, remembering that he is the devil. Just because he gave me food, that does not make him a good guy. I know for sure, he is anything but.

As I walk up the stairs behind him, his round ass fills my view.

He has a nice ass, toned and tight.

This man is good-looking—he may be the most handsome guy I've ever seen.

He halts at a door and opens it. I stop next to

him, unsure, and he nods to the room beyond. I step in to find a television and a bed. I'm too excited to be sleeping in a bed that looks like it wasn't pulled from the dump—with fresh sheets—and to see a flatscreen TV that looks brand new, to even realize until it's too late that he's shut the door behind me.

Then he locks it from the outside.

And then he leaves.

Running over to it, I bang and scream his name.

Kyson doesn't come back.

When I see him next, I plan to scratch his eyes out. Villain or not.

Asshole.

SEVEN

Kyson

THAT WOMAN SCREAMED for most of the night until I assume she passed out. And not long after that, I did as well.

I unlock the door this morning, expecting to find her still asleep. Instead, I step back as something flies at my face, hitting me right in the eye. And then I'm kicked in the stomach. The feisty bitch goes to kick me again, this time in my junk, but I'm expecting that from her, and catch her leg before she can even attempt to swing it into position. Spinning her around so her back is to me and my arms are wrapped around her waist, holding her arms down, I growl in her ear, "You threw the toilet brush at me." My eye still stings from the hard hit.

She shrugs. "You locked me in here, asshole."

"It's a nice room with a comfortable bed, a TV, and its own bathroom," I remind her. Her scent registers in my nose, and she smells good. Clean, like some sort of fucking flower. I push her away because I can feel my cock twitch with her being so close.

That can't happen.

Ever.

"So you think you can lock me up? What world are you living in, asshole?"

"My world. And as far as I'm concerned, you are mine until I can figure out what to do with you."

"Do with me?" she asks, shock registering on her face as her mouth forms a perfect O.

"Yes. Most people don't get the choice. We simply kill them." I turn and leave the bedroom.

"So you're deciding whether to kill me or not?" she asks, and I can hear the fear in her voice.

"Pretty much. So stop throwing shit at me," I tell her, walking down the stairs.

Kalilah follows, her footsteps light. She's still dressed in that god-awful outfit, but at least she smells better now.

"Pancakes, dear," Nancy chirps, and I shake my

head at her. She already has my egg whites and fruit laid out for me. I sit down at the same time Kalilah enters the kitchen. She steps up to Nancy and throws her arms around her. I raise a brow at Nancy, who just hugs her back before Kalilah steps away and comes to the table.

"If I cooked, you think you would suck my cock?" I ask Kalilah.

She isn't shocked by my comment. Instead, she picks up a spoon and throws it at me from across the table while muttering, "Pig." I manage to dodge it and shrug my shoulders before I start eating.

"What am I expected to do today?" she asks.

"Stay here. If you run, I'll hunt you down."

Nancy places two coffees down before she retreats.

"Why do you have Nancy when she should be off living her best life?"

"I killed her husband," I answer truthfully.

Kalilah's mouth falls open, and her hands freeze halfway to her coffee cup. "You what?"

"I killed her husband," I repeat. She looks over her shoulder to see Nancy humming as she cooks. She does love to cook.

"Aren't you afraid she'll, like...try to poison you?" she whispers.

Raising a brow at her, I ask, "You think Nancy would poison me?"

"Well, no, but…you did kill her husband."

"Eat before your pancakes get cold. I have to go clean up your damn mess." Looking back down at my food, I've suddenly lost my appetite. Standing, I walk into the kitchen with my plate and put it on the counter.

Nancy glances at it before she raises her eyes. "You aren't hungry?"

"You aren't trying to poison me, are you?" I ask Nancy.

I hear Kalilah almost choke on whatever she's eating.

"Well, if I were, would I admit to it?" I watch a slow smile cross Nancy's face.

Nodding my head, I grab my shit and leave.

"You took her to your house?" Zuko says, shaking his head in disbelief.

"Can I meet her?" Alaska asks. She's changed the color of her hair again—she tells us it depends on her mood. Today it's red because she feels like fire.

"Why on earth would you want to meet her?" I ask.

"Seems like she's around to stay." We both look at her, confused. "You'll get it soon. Just wait."

"No, I *will not*."

Alaska leans over my shoulder and says, "Pass me your keys and tell me your passcode. I'm going to visit her." She holds out her hand in front of my face.

"You allowing this?" I ask my brother. He shrugs. Clearly, he's whipped by all things Alaska.

"Fucking hell." I pass her the keys and tell her the code. Alaska smiles and walks out the door. "Don't corrupt her." Zuko hides his laugh at my words. "I don't know what to do with Kalilah."

"Well, for starters… Try *not* dropping her on her face again."

"Now, that's some great advice. Not," I say.

"You should ask Kenzo for advice," he tells me.

"He's always busy."

"We all are. Ask him," he orders me.

"Maybe tomorrow," I reply as I head out.

"Don't kill her…yet," he calls out.

"I make no promises," I yell back before closing the door.

EIGHT

Kalilah

SHE HAS red hair and is loud.

And bossy.

She storms in like she owns the place but also seems to have never been here. I'm not sure what to make of it. Or what to say. She eyes me like she's trying to work me out, and not in a good way. At least, I don't think so.

"I'm Alaska, and you are *not* what I was expecting. How old are you?" she asks, eyeing me.

"Twenty-three," I answer.

"Well, okay, I assumed younger. It's good to know you're at least legal, and I don't have to go and beat his ass."

"You could do that? Beat his ass?" I ask, surprised.

Alaska's hand lands on her hip, and she smiles at me. "I'm dating his older brother, so of course I can." She smirks. "I kick his ass when he annoys me too."

She walks to the living room, drops onto the couch, and turns the television on. "So, why are you here?" she asks.

I stand there awkwardly for a moment before I join her in the living room.

"He forced me to be here," I inform her.

"Hmm…" Alaska eyes me. "I didn't take you for his type, but I could be wrong."

"I am *not* his type. I've seen his ex… We look nothing alike." I push my brown hair behind my ear before I take a seat. "Plus, he's an absolute ass to me," I add.

"Yeah, I have a feeling that's how Kyson is." Alaska smiles as she tucks her legs under her ass and puts on some reality television. I briefly wonder how Kyson will feel about Alaska's shoes being on the cream sofa, but then hide a smirk, thinking he'll probably have a heart attack if there are any stains on the fabric.

We sit here for a good hour or two before Kyson arrives home. He takes one look at us and shakes his head before he walks over and grabs the remote from Alaska. She hits him on the back of the head after she gets up, tells me goodbye, and leaves.

Disappointingly, there's not a single remark about shoes being on the furniture.

"You getting people to watch me now?" I ask Kyson as he changes the channel. He puts on a movie—an action-adventure—and doesn't even spare me another glance.

Nancy has been floating around all day, but I didn't bother her while Alaska was here. Now, I get up and leave him to his movie, walking into the kitchen to find Nancy humming as she cooks. She smiles when she sees me and offers me a cupcake she baked.

"Can I ask you something?" I question in a quiet tone, running my fingers along the stone island. Nancy nods her head. "Why do you work here if he killed your husband?"

"My husband hired the boys to kill me." She smirks as she continues, "I met Kyson when he was scoping out my place. I walked outside... No, hobbled would be more accurate, and he saw my black, swollen eyes. I didn't want to tell him the truth, but I did anyway for some reason. I told him I got them when I didn't cook the steak right for my husband.

"Now, usually, I keep that locked up tight. I was accustomed to the abuse by then, as we were married for almost forty years. But that day, I was tired, and a nice young man was showing concern and asking me how it happened.

"I knew my husband was seeing someone else and had been for many years. He started coming home less and less. And when he did show up, it was only to beat me. So I was at my wit's end. And I blurted all this out to Kyson.

"He looked...well, like he knew. Not shocked, which was what I had expected. Then he got angry and left. The next day, my husband was found dead." She shrugs, turns over whatever it is she's cooking, and softly smiles.

"When Kyson returned the next day, I asked him what he did for a living. He told me point-blank, 'I kill people. Your husband was my most recent job.' I was so shocked by this I started crying and he didn't know what to do.

"I begged him to let me pay him back. He, of course, told me no, but I felt freer than I ever had before. And that's all thanks to that man out there. I know he's scary and cold, but he is also amazing."

She starts plating up food as she talks. "One of my favorite things is to cook, so I asked him if I could cook for him. He was confused, not sure what to make of my request. But with time and a lot of pestering, he let me. Mr. Hunter loves my food so much he now pays me, and very well, I might add. He lets me stay in the guest house, and I *am* currently living my best life. Thanks to him."

Well, I didn't expect her to tell me that. I turn back to the living room, where he's still sitting and watching some action movie where they're trying to kill everyone.

"He's never brought a woman back here after that last one. What was her name? Oh, yes, Lilly." I know that name. She's the one who got married. "Though I'm not sure how serious either of them were. I think she wanted more than he could give." I watch as she plates up Kyson's food and walks it out to him. She taps him on the shoulder and hands him the plate. He doesn't say thank you, but she smiles anyway before she returns to the kitchen.

"Hungry, dear?"

I nod and turn around. Kyson's watching me, and I shiver and look away before I say anything I will regret.

"How long do you expect me to stay here?" I ask Kyson a few days later.

He takes in what I'm wearing. Not in an appraising way, just like he's looking at something uninteresting, such as a new potted plant he found in his home. Nancy left clothes on the bed for me on my second night and told me to keep them. They're nice. A little big on me but still nicer quality than anything I have worn recently.

"What do you think you will do, get drunk, roam the streets, and pass out? I'm sure being here isn't hurting you. *Yet.*" He adds that last word with a sinister grin as he runs his hands over his bowtie and fixes it. He's dressed in a suit and looks incredibly good.

"Where are you going?" I ask, ignoring his dig at me.

"Out."

"Can I come?" Lord knows why I ask, but I need out of this house, even if it is beautiful.

He eyes me up and down. "Not dressed like that."

"I'll change. Wait…" I run up the stairs to "my" room and find the pile of clothes. I found a long, black slip dress in there earlier. Even though it's too big for me, the back part ties with a bow, so I just have to pull it tighter. I think your back is supposed to be exposed when you wear it, but mine won't be because of the dress's size. After slipping it on, I find my old, beaten-up heels I wore to most events where I would steal food and slip them on. Then I run my hands down my hair, tie it back into a messy bun, and pull a few strands out to fall around my face.

Done.

When I meet him by the door, I find him checking his wrist for the time.

"I'm ready," I announce, and his eyes glide over my body before they reach my eyes.

"You have no makeup on," he states.

I touch my face. "I don't own any," I answer.

He huffs before he walks out the door. "Best fucking behavior, or next time I'll push you off a cliff."

"Have a great night," Nancy says. As she approaches me, she reaches into her pocket and hands me something. I take it, and when I open my palm, there's a tube of bright-red lipstick. I thank her and hurry out to the car, where Kyson is waiting. He drives in silence, and I flip down the sun visor and use the tiny mirror while I apply the lipstick. Rolling my lips together with a pop, I turn to show Kyson. "Better?" I ask him.

He cracks his neck as he pulls to a stop, not bothering to answer or even looking my way. When he gets out, I do the same, walking around the car to stand next to him.

"Don't talk to anyone," he orders, and those haunted eyes find mine.

"What if someone says hello? Am I supposed to pretend I can't hear them?" I ask.

"Don't be a smartass," he grumbles, walking ahead of me.

As I take in our surroundings, I see a lot of people dressed nicely, it makes me want to tug at my clothes self-consciously, but I resist the urge. *Damn, I'm way underdressed.*

I follow him inside to an opulent, lush-carpeted, chandeliered room where waiters walk around with polished silver trays plated with food. I take a small burger slider from the first one and waste no time putting it in my mouth.

"Do you have to eat everything you see?"

I don't even bother covering my mouth as I smile at him. He rolls his eyes, and I go to reach for a second, but he grabs my hand and puts it down at my side. Then he reaches for the tray of champagne and hands me a glass.

"So I can drink but not eat," I say, nodding. "You have some weird logic."

Kyson ignores me as someone calls his name and starts talking to him. I stand there watching him but not listening because I couldn't care less.

"That dress looks awfully familiar." I turn to a woman I recognize. It takes me a moment to place her, but the last time I saw her, she was in a white dress. "Kyson's date, correct?" she asks, raising her glass to her lips and taking a small sip. I do the same as we stare at each other. "Actually, I think that's my dress. The very same one Kyson tore from me before he fucked me. He never gave it back." I'm not sure what she's trying to prove here.

Is she trying to upset me?

Make me jealous?

Because I sure as shit ain't fucking him.

But good on her for doing so.

Pulling the glass away from her lips, she puckers them and glances over me. "Looked better on me."

"I can see why you were together," I say, just as I feel him come up next me. "You are both cunts." I smile and walk away.

Stepping up to the bar, I lean in and wave the

bartender down. When he reaches me, I say, "Two shots of tequila, please." He raises a brow, and I see that all he's serving is champagne. "You do have some stashed back there, right?"

"Umm...yeah."

"Well, I want it." He stands there unsure at first, shifting from foot to foot, but when I don't move, he reaches under the bar and pulls out a bottle. I don't even know why we're here or what this event is for. But I do know I want *all* the drinks.

I've found that in my life, alcohol helps numb the pain of everything.

And I need a lot of numbing.

"Do you plan to get drunk and pass out again, looking like trash?" Kyson asks from behind me.

"Did you know I was wearing *her* dress?" I ask, not bothering to look at him.

"Yes, of course I did. I bought it for her after all."

"It looks better on me," I add, even though I know that's a lie because I hardly fill it out, where she has a damn dream body.

The bartender comes back with my shots, and I shoot a happy smile at him. Taking one straight away, I go to reach for the second, only to see it disappear before my very eyes.

71

Kyson throws it over his shoulder, and my eyes go wide. He just threw away perfectly good alcohol. Asshole.

"Why are we even here?" I mumble. "You kill people. Why do you need to socialize?" I grumble.

He gets right in my face. "Learn to keep your mouth shut. Or I'll shut it for you," he replies through gritted teeth before he storms off.

I turn back to the bar and order more shots.

NINE

Kyson
___

THAT WOMAN WILL BE the death of me.

Why haven't I killed her yet? That's a good question. She should be six feet underground, yet she still breathes, drinking way too much at the bar.

She knows better than to run, at least, I think she does. So I walk away, not wanting to be around her intoxicating scent.

"Why are you with her?" Lilly asks.

I refrain from rolling my eyes, having excused myself from Lilly to go check on Kalilah when she came up to me earlier. And now she's back.

"Where is your husband, Lilly?"

She waves a hand around. "Who knows? So why are you with her? We both know it will never last. I'm the only one who's come close to lasting with you."

She isn't wrong. I contemplated a lot of things with Lilly. But in the end, I didn't love her the way she wanted to be loved.

And she knew who I was. And didn't have an issue with it.

"Is she even old enough?" Lilly scoffs, drinking the last of her champagne.

"She is." I look past her in the hope she will shut up.

I hate these events, but out of the three of us brothers, I'm the sociable one. The brother our clients feel more comfortable approaching. And that's saying a lot.

Zuko hates people, and Kenzo hardly talks to anyone but Zuko and me.

I've contemplated just sticking to this part of the job. I technically don't need to do this. Our name is enough of a draw for those who want someone to disappear. But it's nice to find the rich ones who are willing to pay incredible amounts of money, and I'm not even sure my brothers know I do this; as in drum up business in this crazy, messed-up affluent world.

"Well, you could do better. That's all I'm

saying," she says.

My eyes find Lilly again, and I lean in real close. "Do you want to go to the back room, Lilly?" Her cheeks flush at my words. Getting close to her ear, I touch it softly with my lips. "Do you want me eating you out while you silently scream my name into a pillow knowing your husband is on the other side of the door, not having any idea what you are up to? Is that something you want?"

"Aren't you married?" I pull back at the sound of Kalilah's voice. She is now standing next to me, her eyes glassy from obviously having too many shots. She waves a finger at both of us. "If I were married, I wouldn't let a man I've fucked before and still have eyes for come that close to me. Does your husband know you want to fuck him?"

"How dare you?" Lilly says as her husband steps over.

"How dare she what?" he asks, sliding his arm around Lilly's waist in a protective movement only a newlywed husband can pull off.

I turn to Lilly to see her eyes wide and on me.

"Your wife still wants to fuck Kyson. Did you know?" Kalilah blurts out.

At first, we all stay silent. Then Lilly's husband's

eyes find mine, anger evident in them before he turns to look at Kalilah.

"You have some nerve, coming in here making accusations," he seethes.

"But...are they accusations?" Kalilah argues with him.

Lilly huffs like she can't believe the nerve of her. Neither can I. But really, I should have known. She has been sassy since the day I met her. Why would she change now?

"Why don't you ask your wife what she thinks?" Kalilah lifts a clear glass of liquid—my guess is more tequila—to her lips and smiles.

He shoots me a look before he turns to his wife and studies her for a moment. Then he addresses Kalilah. "You need to leave," he tells her.

"Oh, do you own this place?" Kalilah fires back but in a mocking tone.

He turns back to me and asks, "This the kind of company you keep?"

I want to laugh because, really, it is funny. And Kalilah can be many things as I am soon coming to realize, but taking orders from men is not in her vocabulary. And when she is a smart ass, when it's not directed at me, it's quite amusing.

"She's right, just so you're aware," I say to him.

"Boom, bitch!" Kalilah yells, dropping her fist as if she dropped a bomb. "Now, put a leash on your wife."

People's attention starts to drift our way with Kalilah's loud mouth. I place my hand on her lower back and direct her to the bar. I reach for the water and pour her a glass and swap the shot glass she has for the fresh water.

"That's my drink," she complains.

"You've had enough."

"Uh-oh." As she says that, I feel Lilly's husband come up behind me. I step to the side just as he swings, and he hits nothing but air. The idiot goes to swing at me again but trips, and as he falls, he pushes Kalilah hard, her back hitting the bar, and I hear a loud crack.

"You whore!" he yells.

"Kyson, please don't. He didn't mean it." Lilly is now beside me, her hand on my arm in an attempt to placate me.

"Don't you dare beg him. It's him who should be worried," her husband snaps.

I step away from Lilly and catch his hand mid-throw. With a quick movement, I turn him around, moving him like a ragdoll until his arm is behind his back, and so am I, then apply pressure, wanting to break his arm. "*You...ever*...lay a hand on Kalilah again... I. Will. End. You. I promise you that. Let your wife fill you in on my promises. Now, control your wife, and leave Kalilah out of it."

Before I let him go, I glance up at Kalilah, who's bent over in pain. "Fuck it." I reach for his pinkie finger and snap it. He screams loud. The music in the place seems to die at that moment, and I let him fall so he can cradle his now broken pinkie.

"Kyson, I don't want to cause a scene, but..." the owner of the event says. "I saw what happened. And I apologize for letting him in."

Lilly's husband screams at her words. She was one of our first clients and is extremely wealthy. She wanted us to kill her cheating husband, who was blowing all her money on drugs and women. It was easily done. So she lets us—me—come to these events to mingle, and I've never caused a scene. People here have more money than sense, and I guess Lilly is now in that category since she married that tool. I don't even remember his fucking name, that's how much I don't care about him.

"He should be out, not me," he yells as people escort the idiot out.

The music starts again and people turn away.

Lady McBeth, who runs this place, steps over and helps Kalilah stand. She gets up with a wince.

"I'm so sorry, dear. Please let me make it up to you. What can I do?" Kalilah looks at me, unsure of what to say. "Anything. You name what you need, and I am here to help." She stands there with her manicured hands clasped in front of her. Not a single hair is out of place, even though I know she must be slightly rattled by what just went down while she waits patiently for Kalilah to answer her.

I nod to Kalilah to let her know she can ask her anything.

What will she ask for?

Money? She's clearly broke.

A place to stay that isn't mine?

I wait to see what she says, and what comes out of her mouth shocks me.

"I'd like a job if you know of anyone hiring," she replies, and I can tell she's in pain, but she covers it well. The mark on her face from where I dropped her is almost healed and looks like a scar that was already there.

Lady McBeth smiles happily. "That's easily done." She hands her a business card which seems to appear from thin air. "Here is my number. You call tomorrow, and Edward will set you up."

"Thank you," Kalilah says, looking down at the card.

Lady McBeth touches my shoulder briefly as she passes me to go back to her guests, who I know will ask what happened, but she will brush it off like it was nothing. She is good at business, that one, and knows precisely how to act and what to say when an incident regarding disruption of her guests occurs.

TEN

Kalilah

"NOW YOU DECIDE TO BE QUIET?" he questions as we walk out to the curb where his car is waiting. The valet holds the door open for me as I get in.

"I'm getting a job," I say in surprise. How long have I been trying to find one, and all it took was one too many tequilas, getting knocked around, and a killer for hire.

I'm getting a job.

I don't even care what it is.

And I just can't stop smiling.

"How's your back?" Kyson asks. I turn in my seat to face him. It hurts, but only a little. Happiness overshadows the pain.

"I'll survive."

"That seems to be your motto," he grumbles.

"Thanks for defending my honor." I smile, knowing full well it wasn't for me but because he's probably jealous.

"Shut up."

"Oh yeah, that's how all the ladies want to be spoken to," I say with an eye roll.

"You ain't no lady."

I flip my hair over my shoulder. "I totally am."

"You keep telling yourself that," he mumbles.

I don't bother arguing with him. What's the point? I have a feeling Kyson usually wins. That or he isn't used to people arguing with him. And to be honest, my back really does hurt, especially now that the alcohol is wearing off.

When we arrive back at Kyson's house, I gasp in pain as I get out of the car, but I don't tell him that. He doesn't bother waiting for me as he walks ahead and into the house, but he does leave the door open. When I get to the stairs, I sit down on them.

Goddammit! My back is really hurting now. Aching.

"Why are you sitting out here?" I don't answer him. Just put my hand on my back and groan. I feel him lean down and touch my back. I don't even bother shooing him away, letting him untie the bow and part the two halves of my dress. "Fucking hell, you said it was fine."

"It was," I tell him.

"Clearly, it's not. Your back is fucking red and bruised." Without another word, he scoops me up as if I'm a child and carries me inside.

"I can walk, just so you're aware," I inform him. Then I scrunch my nose and tell him, "You smell." He does smell, but it's absolutely delicious. So it's best he puts me down because no woman should be subjected to that scent.

He glances down at me, then back up, holding me in his arms as if I am as light as a feather, and I don't avert my eyes from him.

"Stop staring," he says and adjusts his hold on me. I wince and look away. "Fucking hell, you'll have to ice it." He kicks my bedroom door open and carries me to the bed before he gently lays me down. Glancing up at him, I notice he won't look my way. He watches where he puts me before he turns and walks out of the room without saying a word. Sitting up, I let the dress fall from my shoulders and pool at my waist—I have no bra on, as one wasn't needed with this dress—then I try to look at my back. I can't see anything, but I can feel the pain when I twist.

Maybe this week is just that for me—*pain*.

But on the bright side, I'm in a place where it doesn't stink, and no one is going to come in and try to hurt me. Well, that I'm aware of. Managing to get up, I go over to the full-length mirror and turn around so I can look over my shoulder to see how bad it is.

Shit.

It's red.

But then again, I've had worse.

"You have small tits." Whipping my head around, I see him standing at the door with a bag of ice in his hand. After a moment, he enters the room and moves behind me. He lifts the bag and places it on my back. I suck in a breath at his touch and the coldness of the ice against my skin. When I glance back at him, his eyes meet mine.

"Nothing wrong with small tits," I tell him.

Kyson's lips fight a smile, but he says nothing, just holds the bag to my back. I should care that he's in the room with me while I'm half exposed, but he doesn't give me a vibe that I need to cover up around him. Which is weird, considering who he is and what he's done to me.

"I think I've got it from here." I lift my hand and try to reach for the bag, but it hurts to put my arms in that position.

"Lie on the bed… And take that fucking dress off so I can burn it."

I let the dress slip over my hips, and then I walk to the bed. Lying down in only a G-string, I feel something against my skin. Turning my head slightly, I can just see his features. His eyes are trained on my bare ass as he lays a towel on my back, then places the ice. "Go to fucking sleep," he grumbles, throwing the sheet over me before he storms off.

I lie there confused.

What just happened?

My back is aching at a whole new level of pain.

I don't even want to move—that's how much it hurts. I hear footsteps, but my face is smushed into the pillow, and I'm too sore to shift my head to see who it is.

"Fucking hell," Kyson says before I feel his hands on me, then something cold settles on my back. The relief is slight and not enough. I hear his footsteps retreat, and he's gone for a minute before he's back again and says, "You need to move to take these."

"I don't want to," I whine.

"You move on your own, or I move you." I know he means it, so I shift slowly until I'm on my side. The sheet that he threw over me is still slightly covering me, and the ice pack has fallen to the side, but I can still feel it against my back. "Take these. They will help the pain and inflammation." He holds out a couple of tablets as well as a glass of water.

"I can't take tablets," I tell him.

"What do you mean? I've watched you drink. You have no problem with swallowing things that aren't good for you."

"I can't take them. They don't go down, and then I throw up."

He places the water on the bedside table as he grips the tablets. "Fucking hell," he mutters before he stomps out of the room. I stay where I am, unsure of what to do.

Kyson comes back a few minutes later with a spoon and a bottle of honey. "Open," he commands. I look at him, confused. "You said you can't take tablets. I Googled how to make it easier.

Honey and crushed tablets work, so open." I do as he says, and he slides the spoon into my mouth, then he pulls it back out, and I swallow. He hands me the water, and I manage to take a sip before he takes it away. "I have to work, so roll back over," he instructs me.

"You can go to work. I need to pee," I inform him.

"How do you expect to do that? You can hardly move as it is," he grumbles, and I hide the smile that wants to appear as he looks me up and down.

"I'll figure it out."

"Fucking hell," he mutters again.

"That must be your favorite phrase," I tease.

"Only with you," he says. Then he moves to the other side of the bed, and I feel him remove the sheet and place his hands under my knees. "Lift slightly, I'm turning you." I do as he says so my back won't get dragged against the mattress. When my legs are dangling from the bed, he reaches over me, ignoring my still-exposed tits. Instead, he places a hand behind my head and gently helps me up without touching my back but relieving all the pressure from it at the same time.

"You should put on a nurse's outfit... It would look cute."

"I can drop you," he utters, and I can't help the small laugh that leaves me. But I regret it right away because it hurts, and I stop to wince. "Just shut the fuck up," he says, offering me his arm. "And stand so you can piss, and I can leave. You stink of alcohol."

"I'd like a sponge bath if you're offering."

"And I'd like you to suck my cock just so you'll shut up, but hey, this is where we're at."

"Maybe when I'm better, but only if it's pretty. Some men have really ugly dicks."

He mutters something under his breath, and I don't pay him attention as we hobble to the bathroom. He places one of my hands on the wall, stands in front of me, and tears off my G-string. I watch in shock as it falls to the floor.

"I have a handsome cock, and you need new underwear," he says, walking out.

I sit down and pee, and damn, it feels good. As soon as I'm done, he comes back in holding a shirt. He gives me a slight nod to indicate for me to lift my arms.

"What are you doing with me?" I ask.

"Dressing you because you are hopeless."

"How old are you?" I ask.

Kyson gets the shirt over my arms and head,

then pulls it over my breasts until it covers my torso. He steps back and looks down at me; a part of me wants to cover myself but the other part says fuck it. Here is this man, that somehow, even in all the pain I am in, I can somehow still feel my stomach flutter when he touches me, and I hate it.

"Thirty," he replies.

"Hmm..."

"What?" He hands me toilet paper, and I wince as I wipe. He motions for me to stand, and I do so on shaky legs. "You have a hairy bush," he states.

"I haven't found anyone good enough to shave it for." I glance down. "My legs are hairy too. I need to buy a razor, which I can do now that I have a job." I smile proudly.

"You don't yet. Have you called Edward?" My eyes feel heavy, and my back starts to feel a little looser.

"No, but I will," I say, yawning.

When I look down, I see I'm wearing a Harley Davidson shirt. "This yours?" I ask as he helps me back to the bed and instructs me to turn onto my stomach. I do as he says, and he places the ice pack on my back once again.

"Kyson?"

"What?"

"Do you plan to kill me?"

"I haven't decided," he says as my eyes struggle to stay open.

"What *have* you decided?" I ask.

"That you are trouble. A nuisance. And a pain in my ass."

"Yeah, I think the same about you."

"And you have a drinking problem."

"I have a life problem. Sometimes that problem needs to be numbed."

"What are you running from?" he asks.

"Him," is all I manage to say before I can't fight it anymore and sleep takes me.

ELEVEN

Kyson

HIM? What does that even mean? I've got no fucking idea. I know from Kenzo's search that she's running from something, but I have no idea what. And she isn't willingly share information.

I'm standing in the foyer of Pops's house. He's the man who trained us to be his own personal killing machines. He was a trainer for special ops but left to do what he does best—train killers, and we're his first successful killers. So much so he didn't need to find any others. He gave up training more and completely focused on us three. He's money hungry as fuck, which only adds to his intense focus. I know he doesn't like the fact that we don't solely use him to get clients anymore, but he can't do anything about it. Yes, he still brings us the occasional job, but it's up to us if we choose to do it or not.

We were raised differently from a lot of other kids. The streets and each other were all we had. It was fine. We survived. And I think it made us stronger. But I think someone has told Pops I've been having feelings of wanting to leave, and it's why he's called me here today.

"How are you?" Pops asks, handing me a glass. I take it but don't drink. He puts his own glass to his lips. "Let's go into the sitting area. It's just us. No one else is here."

I nod and follow him. When he sits on one of his white sofas, I do the same opposite of him.

"You've been off." *That's how he chooses to start, right.*

"All my jobs have been completed to perfection," I remind him.

"What about her?" He doesn't have to say her name for me to know he's talking about Kalilah.

"What about her?" I ask.

"Kenzo let it slip you didn't kill her."

"Why would I do that?"

"You know there is not to be any sort of evidence or loose ends. We have done a great job at keeping everything clean for this long, so why would you jeopardize that? For a woman?"

"Is this the *real* reason you called me over?" I ask, placing the drink down on the table between us. His gaze flicks to it, but he doesn't say anything. "And leave her out of it. I have it handled."

"Do you?" he asks.

"When have I not?"

"Kyson, out of the three of you, you are the one who talks to me the most. But you've been silent for some time now. Do I have to worry?" He leans in as he says the words with his eyebrow raised in question.

"I'm just working out how to be a better me."

"What's wrong with the 'now' you?" he bites back. "You are amazing at everything you do. You have a charisma about you that your brothers admire. Heck, even I admire it. So tell me, what's wrong?" Pops is the closest thing to a father figure we have. I don't even remember our real father, and as far as we are concerned, we have no other family. Which sits well with us—we don't need much.

"Why does something have to be wrong?"

"Kyson. Tell me."

I contemplate confiding in him. But I'm not sure what to tell him, so I keep it to myself. Zuko was the only one who knew, and now Kenzo does. But that's it. That's all the people who need to know. They don't need me. They do just fine by themselves.

"Fine." He hands me a piece of paper that disintegrates when it touches water. I look over the information and note the address and name. "Your brothers have plans, but I need this job done for a favor I owe."

"Who's the favor for?" I ask.

His head drops to the side as he studies me. "Why are you asking?" He's right to question me. We never question a hunt, but as I said, things are changing.

"Is it a secret? You said it was a favor. I'm asking for who…" I pause, then continue, "Or is this one a secret as well?"

Pops is good at keeping secrets and has been for as long as I can remember.

A woman comes out from the hallway, and I don't recognize her, which isn't unusual. I never know who Pops has in his bed as he goes through so many women. Pops's salt and pepper hair looks good on him, and the women he brings back all seem to love him. She waves as she walks past us, but his eyes remain firmly on me.

"It's not a secret. The governor wants him dead. The mark has been going around saying he will be running next year and will most likely win with all the dirt he has on the governor. So, if you wouldn't mind, I owe him a favor. Or would you like me to get your brothers in on it as well?"

I shake my head in answer, stand, and put the paper in my pocket.

Then I leave without either of us saying another word.

It doesn't take me long to find the mark. He's at a well-known restaurant not far from his apartment. He lives alone. Never been married. No kids. I can do the searching without Kenzo, but he's better—I find basics, and he finds everything.

I watch him for a bit as he sits there drinking. He smiles when appropriate but seems to have a lost look in his eye. Walking past the restaurant, I head straight to his apartment. A man buzzes himself in, and I slip in behind him, making my way to apartment number three. I jimmy the lock, and it opens easily. The place is basic, with creams and whites everywhere. It's small, but I guess that's all you need when you live by yourself.

Why do I have such a big house, then? Because I want it, plain and simple.

Opening his bedroom door, his bed is unmade, and clothes have been thrown around. Shutting the door, I go to the window to check when he leaves the restaurant. I make my way to the door and wait. It's not long until I hear the jingle of his keys, and he enters the apartment.

I hit him on the back of his head, and he falls hard and fast. Shutting the door behind him, I pick the mark up and place him in a dining room chair. Tying his hands behind him, I grab another chair and straddle it in front of him, waiting for him to wake. It takes his groggy mind a few minutes until he starts struggling, and when he stops, his eyes lock on me.

"Hello." I smile. He tries to move back, but he can't. "Just stay still," I tell him. I watch him try to place me, but he won't be able to. I don't know him, and those who know me know better than to show pictures of my face.

"Hunter."

Tickle me pink, I was fucking wrong.

"So, you do know who I am. Interesting." I

smile. "Do you know which one I am?" I ask.

He shakes his head and tries to wriggle himself loose.

"I'd kill you before you got your hands free," I warn him.

He stops moving. "He wants me dead because I have evidence on them all," he whispers. "Even the person who sent you."

"Sorry, what?" I ask, thinking I didn't hear him right.

"What do they call him on the streets? Um… Pops?" he asks, staring at me and waiting for a reaction. "I have enough dirt to send the force after them."

"Yeah, I'm sure you do." I give him a bored look. Pops makes sure everything is done and disposed of. He is clean, remarkably clean.

"His women. He loves his women," he adds. And he isn't wrong. Pops does love women. "They talk, you know. Some were even sent in to gather evidence."

"Where is it?" I ask, standing.

"You'll let me live?"

"Where is it?" I ask again. "If I have to ask a third time, I'll cut your fingers off."

He nods his head to the kitchen cabinet. I walk

over and swing it open, and all I see are glasses. Swiping them out, they all fall to the floor and smash. The tinkling of glass shattering continues long after I view a small slot in the back. You have to be looking for something to see it. Pushing the wood aside, I pull out a folder of paperwork. Turning back around, I sit down in front of him.

The first thing I see when I open the folder is a picture. You can barely make out the image, but I know it's me and my brothers. I glare at him and see his face redden.

"I wasn't going to use them," he adds. "It's the others I want." He nods to the folder. "Keep going."

I do as he says, rifling through. There's evidence of the governor with what appears to be a teenager. Jesus! What a fuckhead. No wonder he doesn't want this information to get out. She looks barely seventeen, whereas he's easily in his sixties. Then I see Pops right next to him, a smile on his face, and another girl next to him the same age as the other.

"That's not all. Those two girls? They're dead."

Hearing that someone is dead doesn't bother me.

"He framed the detective's son because the son was dating one of those girls," he says. "You killed him, the detective… I'm guessing under Pops's orders. He likes you all to clean up his messes without any of you knowing why." I look at the detective's picture and remember him—he was begging us after he fought hard to get away. Told us he had dirt on everyone. We don't deal with that— we deal with money and death, and we are good at it.

And he is also right—it was on Pops's order we killed him.

"Did you also know he is training again?" he adds, and that makes my head swing to him. Pops quit training killers after us because he told us that we were all he needed.

I guess that's a lie.

"To kill you." He smirks. "It's all in there if you keep going." I stand, lean forward, and kiss his fore-head. I like to stomp my kills to death, but for him, I'll be gentle. Reaching for the knife in my pocket, with a movement so fast he doesn't see it coming, I swing it in his direction and straight across his neck. He bleeds quickly, his eyes wide, and I watch as the light leaves them. Then I get my shit and leave, evidence in hand.

I'll send the pyros to torch the apartment in case there is any more evidence.

TWELVE

Kalilah

KYSON DIDN'T COME BACK that day or that night. But the following day, when I go down to the kitchen, I find him sitting at the table. He has a look of confusion and anger written all over his face, his brows tight as he studies something on the table.

Nancy has been crushing the pain-reliever tablets and giving them to me. I feel better. Still incredibly sore but able to walk now without being in so much pain.

"You get lost when you went out?" I ask him, pulling up the seat next to him.

He doesn't even look at me as he mutters, "You should be in bed."

Nancy places a plate in front of me that is

stacked with pancakes with blueberries in them, and they smell amazing.

"I feel better and am taking it easy. And do I have permission to leave?"

He raises his eyes from the papers in front of him and locks them on me. "Why?"

"I have to see Edward today about a job."

"You're injured."

"I'll be fine. It's just an interview to see what type of job he can find for me," I tell him.

"I'll take you."

"I don't need a babysitter. I'll come back." I huff. "I mean, why wouldn't I? You don't plan to kill me...*yet*, your words, not mine. And I have great food to eat, no weddings I have to sneak into, and a safe and comfy bed. You bet your ass I'm coming back, even if that means putting up with you." I smile and take a huge bite of the fluffy pancakes. His eyes follow the movement before he shakes his head and looks away.

"Do you know how to drive?" he asks.

"I do."

Kyson takes something from his pocket. He places a set of keys on the table, and I see the BMW logo. "You can take the car."

"Wow, you're like my sugar daddy." I smile.

"No, just take the car and don't damage it."

"Fine, whatever. What has your attention anyway? Can I see?"

"No," he barks. I don't bother leaning over, I don't want him to think I am snooping. I want to stay until I no longer can.

I just hope to God he doesn't change his mind and kill me in the meantime.

The interview goes amazing. Edward is super lovely and is willing to put me in so many roles with just one positive word from Lady McBeth. He tells me he runs a lot of her businesses, and if she said to give me a job, it's mine. I choose a job working in one of her high-end retailers, happy to learn the ins and outs if they will train me. Edward brushes it off like it's the easiest thing in the world.

I wish it were.

It's been so long since I've had a job I want to celebrate. But I have no money, and the clothes I'm wearing are items Nancy found for me. They fit, sort of, but the skirt is too loose, and I've had to tie it up to keep it from falling. The shirt was easily fixed, though. I am still wearing Kyson's Harley shirt, but it's tucked up under my bra to look like a half-shirt.

With my uniform in hand, which is basically the brand's clothing, complete with shoes, I pull up to Kyson's, excited to share the news with him and Nancy, but the house is dark. Placing my shoes and my bag of clothes down, I go up the stairs. I don't really know which is his room, as I haven't snooped, but I go to the room next to mine and knock.

"What?" a voice calls from inside the room. I push the door open slightly and hear the shower turn off.

"I have news. I got a job. And I can't wait to start. Do you think I can borrow your car until my first paycheck comes in? Then I can at least afford the bus. I mean, I'll pay you back for gas and such. But I can't right now, as you know. Please?"

I see a shadow appear in the bathroom door-way. I don't have a clear view, but I know the person is naked.

Why would Kyson walk out naked when he knows I am in here?

He steps farther into the light, and as he does, I see that he may look like Kyson, but that is not him. I remember this man slightly from that night but barely. He is covered in ink, and he's looking at me like I'm his next meal. Even though I can tell from the light of the wardrobe that his cock hasn't even twitched.

"I'm sorry, I wasn't aware——"

"Are you fucking my brother?"

Brother? Ah, that makes sense.

"What?"

"We met. You were drunk in the back of our car, but we met. I'm Kenzo."

Oh, yes. I vaguely remember him now. And how they killed that man. Damn, you'd think his face would be forever burned into my memory. I guess trauma and booze do a number on the memory.

"I'm amazed you're still alive if he isn't fucking you," he continues.

"He never told me you are...what? Living here? Driving his car?" He doesn't bother covering up as he steps closer to me. I'm trying incredibly hard to look everywhere but at him. However, it's hard when he's naked and oh, so toned.

"I don't know what I'm doing," I answer truthfully.

"Do you want to fuck him?" he asks, stepping even closer. If his cock were hard, it would touch me right now. I notice small cuts on his body, which you wouldn't see unless he was close because of how much ink covers his body.

And it feels wrong, really wrong, to be this close to him while he's naked.

"I should go." I step away, but he reaches for me, his hand gripping mine. I look down at my hand wrapped in his inked fingers.

"He's probably warned you that we hate when people run." I try to pull my hand free, but he holds my wrist tight. "Do you want to run?" When he says it, a smirk touches his lips.

"Yes," I say, not bothering to hide it.

"Good. That means you have sharp instincts." He lets go of my wrist. "Now, where is my brother?"

"Here." We both turn to see Kyson enter the bedroom. His eyes track me from head to toe, and his lips quirk at the shirt I still have on before his gaze moves to his brother. His jaw locks, and his eyes turn to thin slits. "Why the fuck are you naked?" he growls. Then he turns back to me. "Why the fuck are you in my room?"

"I was coming to tell you the good news, but I found your brother here instead," I tell him. I step back and almost fall, but Kenzo manages to catch me by snaking his arm around my back, and I scream from the pain.

"Fucking let her go." Tears start to leak from my eyes, but I hold back the rest that want to claw their way out. Kenzo removes his hand and lets me go. I smell Kyson in front of me before I see or feel him. "You need more pain medication. Told you, you should have stayed in bed."

I pull away at his all-consuming touch. "It's fine. I'll be fine. Was just the way he caught me."

"You're crying," Kyson says as I wipe my eyes.

"It was just a reaction. I'm fine now."

He walks out without another word.

I turn to face Kenzo, who is standing there, still naked, watching me with curious eyes.

"Interesting," he mumbles, more to himself than me.

"I'm fine." I wave at him.

"Show me your back," he says. I turn around, and he grabs my shirt before I do and lifts it. "You'll heal. But it will take time."

"I know that. I'll be fine."

"Famous last words," he says as he goes into the closet. I hear a few things move around before he comes back out wearing a pair of pants. I look at him now because it doesn't feel as weird as it did when he was naked. His chest, neck, and hands are all covered in ink. It's like he doesn't want any skin left uncovered.

"So, Kalilah, have you told him what you're running from?" he asks, and my eyes open in surprise. "I looked into you a little deeper after he went back to help you." He leans in. "Does he know you're married?" he whispers.

My back straightens at his words, and I don't even think about the pain.

"I take that as a no. You better tell him before I do."

Just as he finishes talking, Kyson returns with a spoon, and I know my medicine is on it mixed with honey. He doesn't even hand it to me, just puts it in front of my mouth, and I open for it. He pulls it free when he knows I've swallowed, then he turns to look at his brother.

"Thank fuck you've put on pants. Nancy just started cooking. You staying?"

"Yes." His brother smiles.

"You two look a lot alike," I state.

"Twins," Kenzo supplies.

"Oh." Now it all makes sense.

"Are you having fantasies about fucking twins now?" I quirk a brow at Kyson's question.

"Should I be?" I ask him.

"Are you?" he questions me.

"Is your cock as big as his?" I nod my head to his brother.

"Of course it is." He smirks.

"Nope! No idea whatsoever," I sing as I pass them and go straight to my room. Not long after, Kyson bursts in, holding my things. Shit, I forgot about them.

"What's this?" He holds up the garment bag.

"I got a job. That's my uniform. And I came to ask if I could borrow your car, but you weren't there," I say, biting my lip.

"I'm here, and yes, you can. When do you start?"

"In a few days."

"Are you still thinking about fucking us both?" he asks.

"I said I wasn't interested." I shake my head. "But the more you mention it, the more it will pop into my head." I pause and look at him. "Do you want me to picture it?" and a part of me wants him to say yes. I've been telling myself that I do not like this man, despite how attracted I am to him, and yet here I am. Wanting him to say words I'm not sure I'm prepared to hear.

"Dinner will be ready in ten," he says gruffly, then turns and stalks out.

Not long after Kyson leaves, I see Kenzo pass by my door with a smirk on his face. He nods to me and keeps going.

I lie back on the bed carefully, and all I can think about is how hot both of them would be standing side by side, naked.

Guess I *am* fantasizing about it.

Thank you, Kyson.

Guess I know what I will be dreaming of tonight.

Two Hunters.

But it's only one of them who I want to tie me up and tell me what a good girl I am.

How fucked is that?

For all I know, he is going to kill me, and here I am, hoping he's going to fuck me.

Fuck! I'm fucked.

THIRTEEN

Kyson

"YOU LIKE HER," Kenzo says, and I firmly shake my head. "It's why she's still breathing and driving your car."

"I'd have to agree, Mr. Hunter. He does like her."

"Nancy," I growl, and she simply chuckles and walks back out.

I turn to face Kenzo again. "Why are you here?"

"I finished at the Red Room, and Pops was heading to my house. I figured I would speak to you first before him." I sit back, not sure what to say. He knows I found information on Pops, but he doesn't know the extent of it.

"How often are you going to the red room these

days?" I ask. The Red room is in the sex club our friend, Grayson, owns. The Red room is for blood play—Kenzo likes to cut and be cut.

"Enough. You know my allegiance lies with Pops. Are you telling me it shouldn't?"

"Are you saying you would pick him over me?" I ask, surprised by his word choice— allegiance.

"I'm not saying that, but we all know you have been off lately."

"He sent me on a job the other night," I inform.

"And that's not unusual. Sometimes he asks us to do things by ourselves."

"Fucking rarely," I add.

Pops knows we work better together, cleaner.

"What did you find?" Kenzo asks.

"It's more what the hit said, but yes, what I found too." I place the paperwork on the table with the stack of photographs and keep the other to myself until I decide how to tell them that he is also planning our take down, so it seems. He leans in and studies the evidence. His nose scrunches, and his brows narrow when he sees the images laid out before him, his eyes shooting to mine as he pulls them closer.

"I know her." His words surprise me because I didn't expect him to know anyone in these pictures.

Apart from the one man we killed—the detective. "She's been to Pops's place."

"Did you say anything?" I ask. "Clearly, she's underage."

"I did. Pops told me she was there for her boyfriend."

"Her boyfriend's father, who we killed. Detective Jack. He knew all about Pops," I reply.

"What did he know?" He leans in. "All I see is evidence that Pops likes his women a little younger. It's disgusting, and we should fucking chop his cock off, but that's Pops."

"He sent me there to kill the man because he was going to expose him," I tell Kenzo.

"And?"

"Fucking hell! We don't clean up his messes. We're paid to do other things. He is using us now."

"He probably is." He shrugs.

"You are fucked, you know, that right? We do at least have some standards but by the sound of it you don't?"

He leans in and places his hands on the table. "Why are you on this righteous kick? You need to get off it. We kill. We have no remorse. End. Of. Fucking. Story." He locks eyes with me. "It's the girl, isn't

it? Oh, actually, this started happening before her…"
He pauses, waiting for me to respond. When I don't,
he continues, "It's funny when you think about it.
You were probably the darkest of us all, and yet here
you sit, worried about what Pops is doing."

"It's wrong."

"What we do is wrong," he points out. "You
stomp on people's heads to kill them, but not before
you kiss them. Is that somehow, right?"

"You're missing the point. We don't kill kids.
Even we have our limits," I remind him.

He shrugs. "And for all you know, this is fake."

"You just said you saw her with him. Plus, there
are pictures," I argue. "You should be on my side,
not his." Fucking hell, I want to tear my hair out
right now with this conversation. How is he riding
so fucking hard for Pop's right now.

"I am."

"Why did that not sound convincing?" I ask as
Nancy walks in with our food, ending our
conversation.

Not long after that, Kalilah walks in slowly and
sits between us at the table. Nancy returns and
places Kalilah's plate down and smiles before she
goes back to the kitchen.

"Did you request pancakes again?" I ask Kalilah.

"Yep. Chocolate chip today," she chirps.

"You could use the extra weight," Kenzo grumbles.

"Thanks. I thought the same, but money has been tight, so food is limited."

She takes a bite and turns to me. "Steak and veggies. Is that all you ever eat?" She then glances at Kenzo's plate to see he has the same.

"It's good for you...nutritious," I reply, cutting into mine as Kenzo does the same.

"And it's damn well mooing. Eww... That's gross." She shivers in disgust.

"Mooing?" I ask, confused.

"Yes. It has blood oozing..." She shudders again. "That's just wrong on all levels."

"Blood's never bothered us," Kenzo adds, putting a slide of the steak in his mouth.

"You're both disgusting." She takes another bite of her massive stack of pancakes.

"I can show you something you would appreciate," I tease her. I look down at my lap and back at her.

She tilts her head and scrunches her nose. "Hmm... Even if I wasn't sore, I've already seen your twin, so I'd have to politely decline. And I'm sure you can pay someone to help with that issue." She waves a fork around in my direction before she digs back into her pancakes, and we watch as she sits there eating more than I would think someone her size could consume.

"I don't have to pay for sex," I manage to say, while those eyes find mine and she swallows her mouthful before she speaks again.

"So do you go and fuck your bitch of an ex instead?"

"She is a bitch, isn't she?" Kenzo agrees.

Kalilah turns to him. "Abso-fucking-lutely," she says, then adds, "And she obviously still wants your brother."

"She doesn't," I argue.

"She was willing to fuck you knowing full well her new husband was there." She takes another bite of her pancakes.

"You are *really* getting on my fucking nerves."

"Yeah, yeah." She stands and pushes her now empty plate to the middle of the table. "I have work tomorrow, and I'm taking your car." She spins and walks off, her ass swaying as she goes, and once she's out of sight, I turn to my brother, who's smirking.

"She's different from your usual type," he says.

"Yeah, I'm still contemplating what river I should throw her into next," I mumble.

Kenzo laughs before we sit in silence, eating the rest of our food. He doesn't ask any more about Pops, but his phone rings with a call from him, which he leaves unanswered.

FOURTEEN

Kalilah

SINCE I STARTED my job a week and a bit ago, everyone I work with has been nice, and they are more than happy to teach and show me around. It helps that I look like one of them, not a homeless delinquent. I mean, I have a roof over my head, even though it was forced upon me. *I guess that's better than the alternative, right?*

I've barely seen Kyson since that night with his brother. He left his keys with Nancy and said the car was mine to use. I'm extremely grateful. Not only is his car flashy to drive, but it's also extremely comfortable. The BMW has a ton of power, which makes me feel invincible—even if it's only an illusion. I've never driven something like this before, and the sense of pleasure and luxury is beyond measure. I can only dream of owning something this incredibly desirable.

Pulling into the driveway, I find Kyson sitting out front, his hands on his head as he looks down, lost in thought. I turn off the car and step out and walk slowly over to him.

"I feel like it's been forever since I've seen you," I comment, taking the seat next to him. His head lifts, and his eyes meet mine. I can see pain in their dark depths. *How can a man as beautiful as him have any pain?* That baffles me. "Work has been going well. I get my first paycheck next week." He says nothing, so I raise my face to the night sky, but I know his stare is penetrating me.

"How is your back?" he asks.

"Good. I forget about it most of the time. Though, when I look in the mirror, it's many different colors now." I wince.

"Want to fuck?"

My head swings down and around to face him. *Did he really say that to me?*

"Was that a joke?" I ask, surprised.

Kyson smirks because my answer isn't a straight no, and it seems he knows my answer before I even do. He stands, steps in front of me, and offers me his hand. I stare at it, confused and unsure of what to do.

"Would you like to see how big my cock is? Because I know you've seen my brother's." I cough out a strangled sound, and then I place my hand in his.

I know this will change everything.

We will change.

Whatever it is we are, will change.

He leads me into the house, and it's then I notice he has blood on the back of his hand. I go to pull away, but he notes the direction of my stare and says, "It's my own blood from when I punched the fucking wall." I check his knuckles, and there's large scratches, missing skin, and dried blood.

"Why?" I ask, curious.

He ignores my questions and continues into the house, tugging me behind him.

We pass through the entryway and up the stairs until we get to his room. The door is already open. Kyson drops my hand as he enters, and I stop in the doorway, staring after him. He doesn't bother turning on the bedroom light, but the light coming from his closet falls on his face, which gives me a determined stare.

"I want to fuck hard and rough; do you get it?" Kyson asks, turning to face me. He starts to undo his buttons slowly, all the while waiting for me to reply.

"Rough?" I squeak.

"Yes. I'll be mindful of your back," he states, pulling his shirt off. My eyes track him as he carries it to his closet and hangs it on a hanger. While his back is to me, he kicks off his shoes and places them in the rack before he removes his trousers, draping them neatly on another hanger.

And then he is standing there naked.

Kyson is tanned, his skin olive in complexion and very, very lickable. Not a hair on his back or ass. He turns, and I get my first glimpse of his hard cock.

"You can undress now," he tells me.

I don't. I continue to stare at him until he huffs and walks toward me. He reaches for my uniform and starts to undo the first few buttons. His fingers work quickly and meticulously until my bra is exposed. He reaches for my skirt and unties the side of it, letting it drop to the floor. Kyson lifts his hand to touch my bare stomach between the open halves of my shirt, then trails a finger down to my G-string, where he hooks into it before pulling very slowly and lowering to his knees.

"Maybe we can start soft," he says quietly, and I can't seem to find the words to answer him back as I gape at him. He lifts my feet, one after the other, until my underwear is on the floor, making sure when he puts my feet down that they touch the edges of the doorjamb so I'm spread wide open.

What is happening? I didn't think I would be fucking Kyson anytime soon.

He is, after all, what some might consider too handsome. In contrast, I'm putting weight back on from not having enough food. And yet, the way he's eyeing me, makes me think maybe I've read him wrong all this time.

No, that can't be right.

He dropped me on my face.

He pushed me into the river.

Yet, he is on his knees, his mouth inches away from my unshaven pussy.

I need to buy a razor.

He doesn't seem to mind or care though.

Kyson's finger trails up my thigh until he reaches my center.

I feel myself vibrating with anticipation and need—it has been so long since I've had sex.

The last person I had sex with was my husband,

and frankly, that pleasure was all his, not mine. And that was well over a year ago.

I haven't been attracted to anyone and haven't thought of anyone in that way.

And now there's Kyson.

Dark, malicious, and mysterious.

All the things I should stay away from.

This is madness!

But I have had worse at home. My life was anything but kind to me.

This man shows me that he's far from what I left behind.

Though he probably could decide to wake up tomorrow and murder me.

Hopefully, he'll let me come first. I chuckle inside at the insanity of that thought.

His fingers slide up and down my thighs before he leans forward. My hands grip the doorjamb as his tongue slips out and touches my lips, not the ones on my face. He licks them up and down before he focuses on my clit. I grip the wooden frame a little tighter as he continues, while his other hand slides up my leg and to my opening. He teases my pussy, his fingers moving in torturous circles, applying pressure when needed, before he slips one finger in and out of me.

I think I've died and gone to heaven.

He knows what he's doing.

Who the hell taught him, I wonder.

Or can he somehow read my body better than anyone else?

I'd like to think it's the last option, but you never know.

My head lolls back, and an unbidden memory from the first time I met him flashes through my mind.

Safe word.

I freeze, and Kyson notices. He stops what he's doing and pulls back so his body is away from mine but remains on his knees.

"Are you hurting?" he asks. I shake my head and avoid making eye contact with him. "Then why did you tense up?" His hand shifts to my calf and he rubs lazy circles on it.

"I…"

"Speak, Kalilah."

I open my mouth again as I look down at his hand on my calf. "You use safe words."

"I told you I like it rough," he says. His hand pauses. "But not with you. I know you are injured."

I want to laugh because he has hurt me in the past.

123

"You fell on your own face… I just didn't stop it," he adds, like he knows what I'm thinking. *True, but still, he pushed me into the water.* "I can read you as well as anyone, and the water was to cool you off."

He stands, and I wish he didn't because I did love what he was doing. It was just my mind getting in the way, taking over, as it does so often these days.

"No safe words…" he pauses, "*yet.*" Kyson steps closer and reaches for me. His fingers, the very same ones that were inside me, are now tracing their way up my stomach until they reach my breast. "What safe word would you like?" he asks. "For future reference."

"Why? You don't think you can control yourself?" I sass back.

He gives my nipple a pinch, which I feel right in my core, but I stifle a moan and look up at him. He is so big, so strong, the muscles ripple along his arms. And I know that sounds corny as fuck, but he is one hundred percent alpha male.

He lets go of my nipple, and his hand goes to my chin. With a finger under my chin, he raises my head until I look into his eyes. I see madness swirling around in them, along with anger and a touch of pain.

"I guess time will tell," Kyson says, leaning in.

My gaze moves to his lips as they descend closer to mine. I think he is about to kiss me, and I'm not sure how I feel about that, considering he was just between my legs. But at the last minute, he doesn't kiss me, and his mouth lands on the corner of my lips instead, where he softly says, "Safe word."

"Madness," I whisper.

He pulls back, and a devilish smirk appears on his lips.

"Fitting, I would say."

And I agree.

His eyes trace over me, then he orders, "Get on the bed on your hands and knees."

My husband was controlling in all aspects of my life. So, when Kyson tells me to do something, I want to fight it. I want to kick and scream and tell him to fuck off. But I don't want to compare Kyson to my husband. The problem is it's really hard not to, and getting out of my own head is even harder.

I need to keep reminding myself they are different people. And I should never assume things about people based on the actions of someone else.

With slow and deliberate steps, I walk to his bed. There are white sheets, perfectly crisp and flat, and a blue duvet which has been pulled back. His bed actually appears incredibly comfortable with a pillowy surface.

I glance over my shoulder when I slide my hands over the bedding to see he's watching me with those dark, lustful eyes. He doesn't make me feel self-conscious. In this particular moment, the way he is staring at me makes me feel anything but.

Looking away from him and taking a deep breath, I try to clear all thoughts from my mind because despite how we started out, I actually like where we are. This is crazy and baffling to me because these are *not* normal circumstances.

How did this even come about? Did he save me? Or am I to be his next victim?

I'm not really sure which is the correct answer, but I push the thoughts to the very back of my mind as I crawl onto this bed.

"Deep breath," Kyson says as he comes closer. I feel him behind me even though he isn't touching me yet, but now I'm fully exposed to him.

I hear movement, but I try to keep my eyes trained forward and flinch as he grips my lower hips, careful not to touch my back, and holds me in place. His mouth is between my legs, and his tongue is doing some crazy nonsense down there. I don't even know what to make of it. It's intense and hot and then fast. It's sensory overload as I'm assaulted with every sensation. Before I know it, my back arches, and I throw my head back as I start to move my hips, basically humping his face. He doesn't care, though. He pulls away, and I push back, but he merely blows hot air on me. I push back again, and he chuckles before his mouth is back at it.

Thank you, God.

"I don't think God is who you intend to thank. Maybe you should be worshipping *me*," Kyson says against my pussy.

Damn, I guess I said that aloud.

His words go in one ear and out the other because as soon as he's done talking, his mouth is back against me, and I feel him slip a finger in, but he doesn't put it where I thought he would.

His thumb circles the rim of my asshole before he pushes it in. At the same time, his tongue enters my pussy. My knees give out, and I face plant straight onto the bed, basically doing the splits as I fall. His fingers keep moving, never stopping until I come down from my pleasure high, as if he under-stands my body enough to know to keep finger fucking me until my body stops pulsing. I hear the crackle of a wrapper, and I check over my shoulder to watch him pulling a condom over his impressive length. I'm glad he thought of that because he did precisely what he intended to do—clear my mind—and all I can think now is, *can he make me come again?*

"I'll be as gentle as I can," he says.

I nod, but I don't even know if he sees.

"Stay on your stomach so we don't put pressure on your back." Then his cock is at my entrance, and he meets my eyes before he slides into me and says, "Words. Do you understand?"

"Yes," I reply, as he caresses my ass with his hand, palming it before he smacks it playfully. When he sees my reaction, pushing back toward him, he smacks my ass even harder. I yelp, and he ever so slowly pulls out to the tip and then back in as if he's savoring the moment. There is some discomfort as I adjust to his size, but, oh my God, it feels so good at the same time.

When he's seated all the way inside me, he stops, and I suck in a breath.

"Fuck, you feel good," he says on a groan.

I can't form a reply.

I'm afraid to move.

This feels so good. And tight. And holy shit, he's moving.

Kyson slides out, still slowly, and then repeats

the process. He does this again and again, building a steady rhythm.

"Slap me," I scream, as everything becomes too much. He does, hard, and the sting helps. "Again." He does it again, never stopping his thrusts and keeping that slow and steady pace.

I push back, and I feel myself start to build.

"That's a good girl," he whispers as he feels me tighten around him. "Just a little longer." Kyson slaps my ass again even harder. It smarts, and I know it's going to be sore after, as I feel the sting already. His hands move to my hips, and he starts plowing into me, not holding back. I give a small scream, and one of his hands slips between my legs and finds my swollen, sensitive clit, which he rubs in circles as he continues to fuck me.

Heaven, are you there?

Or maybe it's the devil I should be thanking.

"*Ohhh* my." I can't control the scream that rips from me as he continues to thrust. After he removes his hand from my clit, he slaps my ass again, and I come even harder and stronger.

My elbows start to give out, but he snakes his arm around my torso, holding me up, continuing his steady pounding. Moans and groans that I don't

recognize come from my mouth and fill the otherwise silent room.

How can he...

"Fucking hell." My whole body locks up tight,
but that doesn't stop him as he drives in even
harder. It's not pain I'm feeling. It's my body getting
ready for what's to come. I try to count in my head
to bring myself back down, hoping to prolong this
sweet agony, but the pleasure takes over, and so does
he, picking up his rhythm.

An orgasm tears through my body, and I have
no alternative but to scream his name from my lips.
There's no stopping it.

FIFTEEN

Kyson

I'M NOT sure if she's asleep or dead. Either way, she hasn't moved.

"You're leaking on my bed," I inform her.

Kalilah cracks open one eye and closes it again before she speaks, "Shut up. It's your cum, so what are you complaining about."

"Are you in pain?"

"No, I need to pee, but I can't fathom moving right now."

I've showered, dried myself, and put on boxers, all while she hasn't moved an inch. Her legs are hanging off the bed as she grumbles something unintelligible. I lean over and reach under her arms and lift her back toward me. Her feet touch the ground, and I scoop her up and carry her to the bathroom. She's exhausted and fighting to keep her eyes open. I turn on the shower and wait until it's warm before I place her on a built-in bench. The hot water hits her straight away, and she groans at the comfort it provides her.

"Do you plan to pee or to have me stand here all day?" I ask.

She opens her eyes. "I'm not peeing in front of you again, I barely know you. Last time I had an excuse, I was broken."

"I just ate your cunt, so hurry the fuck up and pee so we can both go to sleep."

"You have such a filthy mouth."

"Didn't hear you complaining when you came," I tell her, crossing my arms over my chest while I stand at the end of the shower outside the spray area. She smirks and pees from her seat on the bench.

"Happy?" she asks.

"Please. Peeing is the last thing you should worry about. I've seen the inside of people's brains. This is nothing. Now, hurry the fuck up." I turn and grab the body wash and squeeze it onto the loofa, then hand her the loofa with the soap bubbled and ready to go.

She smiles as she takes it. "Maybe next time I'll pee in your mouth."

"Don't talk dirty to me." I smirk, and her groggy eyes go wide as she looks at me in shock. "Wash yourself," I order.

She does but keeps an eye on me. "Is that your thing...your kink?" she asks, quieter now. "Because that is *not* something I want to do."

"What if I said it was?" I challenge.

Kalilah thinks it over while she washes herself. "Well..." I wait, and when she looks up, she sees my smile. "You're being a jerk."

"Of course, I don't want you to piss in my mouth. Though I do get that it's a fetish, it isn't one of mine."

"What's yours?" she asks.

"I like to fuck," I reply immediately and move away to get a towel. When I come back, she's where I left her, but she's finishing up rinsing off the soap. I turn the faucet off and step in.

"Do you want to walk?" She shakes her head, so I wrap the towel around her, and she lifts her arms easily. When the towel is secure, I pick her up again.

"I could get used to this. Best treatment I've ever had after a fuck," she mutters.

"What did you do last time?"

"I ran," she says.

I stop dead and stare at her. "What?" I am unsure if I heard her correctly.

"I ran."

"Why?" I take her to the bed and place her down. It doesn't even occur to me that I should have walked Kalilah to her own bed until I climb in after her. She lies on her back and whines when she moves.

"Is it your back?" I ask.

She turns her head toward me. "No, my ass."

I can't help the smile that touches my lips, but then the question that's been roaming around in my mind comes to the front, and I ask, "Why did you run?"

"Because I knew he would pass out after sex. It was the perfect time for me to get the hell away," she whispers.

"Who from?"

"My husband," she admits, dropping a bomb that I didn't see coming. My gaze flicks to her hand that's gripping the towel, and that's when I see the outline of a ring that she must have worn for some time. "I haven't told you because I wasn't sure how..." She pauses. "But now that we've fucked, well, you should know I'm married."

"I've fucked many married women," I point out.

"Yeah, I get it. But—"

"Why did you run and not just leave him?"

"He was controlling. I saved enough money—well, I'll rephrase…hid enough to get me by for a certain amount of time. But no one would hire me because I couldn't use references. I knew if I did, he would find me, and I changed my surname. I've been getting by…barely. But I know he'll be mad, fucking furious, actually, but I don't care. I just want to be free of him."

"Tell me his name."

"No," she says.

"You know I can find it easily."

"Your brother already knows."

My eyes narrow. "Kenzo?" She nods. "Did your husband hurt you?"

"You hurt me," she reminds me, moving her body and wincing.

"You enjoyed that though."

"My face didn't the first time," she scolds.

"I didn't like you then," I say. "So who was I to care if you fell."

"So, you like me now?"

"You're fuckable. Or have you forgotten?" I slide my hand up her towel and touch her pussy.

"No. No way. I'm sore." She pushes my hand away. "Shoo."

I chuckle as I pull my hand away.

"Why was your hand bloody?" she asks, running her finger over the hand that rests on her stomach.

"I've learned some things I'm not happy about," I reply.

"Do you want to share?"

"If I tell you and you leave me or share the information, I will kill you."

"Okay, best not to then." She nods in agreement.

I pull my hand away and look up at the ceiling, silently thinking.

Before I got home, I went to see Pops, and he lied to my face. I asked him if he knew why the last hit was taken, and he gave me the same story as before.

He lied.

He was paying back a favor.

But I think that favor was his own.

A cover-up.

He was mad, furious, that I was even questioning him. It's not something any of us have done previously. We've always trusted his judgment, and maybe we shouldn't have.

We're no angels, far from it, and I'm sure there is a special place in hell for us, but right now, we aren't there.

Pops asked me if I wanted to stop. Said he would stop giving me jobs for a while. That I most likely simply needed a break.

It's interesting because before I found out his dirty little secret, he would be mad as hell at me for wanting to stop, but now he's offering a choice.

Which makes me believe he's hiding something more.

But what?

"I can hear you thinking," she mumbles, her eyes closed and half asleep. She reaches out and places her hand on my bare chest then taps it with her fingertips before she settles her hand flat on me. "Time for sleep. I have work tomorrow, and I would hate to tell them I'm late because I have a sore ass." I laugh and soon hear a small snore leave her mouth. Turning to my side, I watch her, then fall asleep with the shape of her face behind my eyelids.

And I wonder, *Can I kill her husband without her knowing?*

SIXTEEN

Kalilah

WHEN I WAKE, Kyson is not in bed.

My ass is stinging, but I had an amazing sleep. The door opens, and Nancy quietly enters. She's careful not to turn on the light, but I see her kind smile anyway.

"Mr. Hunter asked that I wake you if you didn't wake in time. You have work soon."

"Thanks, Nancy." She stands there for a moment, and I know she's dying to say something else. "What do you want to know, Nancy? Just ask me… I'm not him."

"I want to say this makes me happy." She smiles and waves a hand at the bed before she turns and leaves the room.

Sitting up, I feel the sting straight away on my

ass. Managing to stand, I walk over to the mirror in his mahogany walk-in closet and switch on the light before I turn around to look. His handprints are evident all over my ass. I bite my lip as I study them and remember why I'm so sore everywhere.

In the best way possible.

Who knew sex could be so much fun? Instead of *wham, bam, thank you, ma'am*, which is all I was used to. Now…

"That ass sure does look good." I jump at the sound of his voice but don't bother covering myself. The man's seen me naked, peeing, passed out, and possibly worse. Kyson stalks in, and when I say stalk, I mean exactly that. Dressed in all black, he walks straight over to me, bends down, and before I can figure out what he's doing, his lips are on my ass, and he's placing a soft kiss on it before he stands back up. "I got back early. You were snoring, so I didn't want to wake you." He removes his black jacket and steps past me to hang it up in his walk-in closet.

"My brothers will be over soon, and you have work, so I'd suggest you get out of my sight before I fuck you again. Keys for the car are on the hook near the door." He turns to face me, now in only a black button-up shirt with sleeves rolled up to his elbows. I reach for the jacket he just hung up. Slinging it on, I smile, not saying a word before I saunter out and straight to my room.

Or his room.

Actually, they're all his, but this is the one I have been staying in.

After quickly getting dressed, I fix my face and brush my hair back, pulling it into a high ponytail. I step into the hallway to the sound of talking. At the bottom of the steps are four men. One is Kyson, two are his brothers, and the fourth is a man I don't know, who seems to be a little older. He stares at me intently. I descend the stairs and shoot them a smile as I head for where the car keys hang and pluck them off their hook.

"Have a good day, Kalilah," Kenzo says.

A part of me doesn't want to turn back around, but I smile at Kenzo and nod. Taking one last glance at Kyson, I walk out the door with my head held high.

It's late when I arrive back at Kyson's house.

I stayed a little longer at work for more training in customer service, and I think I finally have it down. Not all of it, because I'm obviously still learning, but I like what I'm doing. I wish I could earn enough to even think about owning half the things these women come in to buy. *Like, what do they do?*

I realized early on that I should never assume it's the husband's money. Over sixty percent of the women who come into the shop are independent and not married. One lady said today, "I buy things because it makes me feel good. Money comes and goes, but that feeling of knowing I earned and deserve what I buy is wonderful." And I smiled at her as I handed her the twenty-thousand-dollar bag and thought how crazy that sounded.

I guess coming from someone who struggles, it would be out of the norm. But for all I know, she may have come from nothing and worked her way up. And why wouldn't you celebrate that? No one will love you as much as you do or celebrate your wins as well as you can.

At least, that's been my experience.

I married Tony when I was eighteen, and from then on, I lived with him and did everything he wanted to do. That included turning away from my family because I believed what he said.

They didn't want us together. And I have since

realized, what person, who loves you wouldn't want your happiness?

I even let him steal from them.

Now that was an all-time low.

Even I know that.

It's why I've never gone back.

Because they know it was me who let him in.

They had locks and passcodes, and the only person who knew them and had access was me.

But Tony said we needed the money.

We didn't, *he* did.

That should have been the first major red flag, but I let it go.

I let a lot of things go.

And I vowed never to do that again.

I want to be in control.

Granted, in this situation right now, I may not be fully in control. But Kyson did save my life and has also rocked my world in the bedroom, so right now, I feel comfortable.

I am not at his house by force. Kyson lets me leave whenever I want without a word.

The day I decided to leave Tony, I knew I was done and that the love we had was fabricated. And all kinds of wrong. He was older than me. My parents told me to wait it out, not marry him straight away, but I was impatient, and as a young girl, you dream about your wedding.

He was offering me the things I dreamed about.

And I jumped.

With both damn feet.

It was okay, not amazing, at the beginning.

But then, when he hit me the first time, a year into our marriage, I tried to leave him, but he got down on both knees and begged me to stay and told me he would change.

It was exactly six weeks after that when he hit me again.

And then again.

And I could see no escape.

Tony was all I had left in this world.

The asshole had told me early on that my friends were shit and that I shouldn't be around such vile people.

He was the vile person.

I was just too late to see that.

And when I finally did, I'd already lost everyone.

So, without him even noticing, I took and sold small things. And if he did notice, I said I broke it. Eventually, I had enough saved to leave, but not before he got one final round in.

The last time we had sex, I would say I was a starfish—still and stiff—but he had the time of his life even though he knew I didn't want to be there. Tony never seemed to mind, though, and I hate him a little more for that.

So, I decided to put away that girl who kept her mouth shut and listened. Now I kick men in the balls and back-talk them. And I like the new me more than the timid girl who was married to Tony, the damn asshole.

She didn't know any better, and it took some learning.

But now, I'm happier. Even though I'm in a state of I-don't-know-what-the-fuck-is-happening.

I'm still happier.

"Kalilah." I pause at that voice.

"Kalilah." And that voice.

I know to whom those voices belong.

With quick steps, I reach to turn on the light in the hallway as I hang up the key. Everything is dark, and I can't hear anyone else. Usually, Nancy is done by this time, but for all I know, she could still be around.

"Leave it. And drop your things." I hear Kyson speak, but I don't listen. Instead, I flick on the light, and when I do, they are sitting in the living room shirtless.

"Um…" I look at them, fumbling a little in confusion before my gaze is drawn to Kyson. "What's going on?"

"Remove your uniform," Kenzo demands.

My eyes go wide as I stare at Kyson, but he says nothing and simply watches. Kenzo starts tapping something in his hand, and it's then I realize he's holding a knife.

Fuck me.

"I wouldn't be afraid of me…*yet*," he says.

For some unknown reason, I don't think he is out to hurt me. I flick my eyes off the knife and look back to Kyson, who sits there, hands in fists on his legs.

"Undress and show him your ass," Kyson orders.

Should I slap myself to see if I'm dreaming? I'm not really sure what's happening right now, and I have to work up the courage to do as he says. Being naked in front of Kyson is fine, but I don't know his brother. Kenzo has always seemed reserved and, might I say, problematic. When you stare into those obscure abysses, you see something deeper in his eyes. Something darker.

"Kalilah, undress."

My back straightens at Kyson's words, and I follow his command. I start by kicking off my shoes, followed by unbuttoning my blouse. Then I turn and shimmy my skirt down my ass so they get the full view, and I'm not entirely sure I want to see both of them staring at me.

"See... You know how to listen."

I don't respond to his taunt. Instead, I hook my G-string with my thumbs and pull it down slowly, bending over as I do.

"Kalilah." I look over my shoulder to Kyson as he says my name. "On all fours and face me." I nod my head and do as he says, then he taps his knee. "Now, crawl to Kenzo. Show him what a good girl you can be." The part of me that was suppressed for so long with my husband wants to fight back, but the thing is, I know I can. With my husband, I knew what came with wanting to fight back.

A punch, a well-placed kick, or something worse.

Kyson gives me a whole different vibe.

He was supposed to kill me, yet he saved me.

He was supposed to lock me up, yet he gave me the key to his car to go to work.

I've been freer with him than I have my whole adult life.

And that in itself, is sad.

So I fucking crawl because I know in the end it will have been *my* choice.

"Your tits have grown since the wedding," Kyson points out. "How you fit a flask between them still baffles me," he adds, never taking his eyes off me. I take each movement toward Kenzo slow and steady. I lift my eyes and see him watching me. There's no smile on his face, but his lust-filled gaze is intently locked on me.

"Careful love, he bites," Kyson says.

And I believe him.

So I stop when I reach Kenzo's shoes and get up on my knees. He opens his legs and I shuffle between them.

"Undo his pants, but don't touch."

I do as Kyson says.

With surprisingly steady hands, I reach for Kenzo's belt and undo it, my hands accidentally touching his lower stomach, and I feel his stomach ripple. When I've released the button and lowered the zipper, I hear Kyson say, "Good girl. Now free his cock."

His impressive length is straining behind his

boxers—it's not like I haven't seen it already, as he freely showed his dick to me the last time he was in Kyson's room. I reach in and grip his cock with my whole hand and squeeze before I pull it out. Kenzo's hips shift almost imperceptibly, and I feel Kyson move in behind me, his hand rubs my bare ass in slow and steady circles.

"Tell me, love, what do you think of his cock?" Kyson asks as he continues rubbing my ass cheek. Each circular motion moves lower and lower toward where I want him to be. I bend, just a little, and he takes the invitation to move even lower. My hand is on Kenzo, but my mind is on where Kyson is touching me.

"Kenzo is not allowed to touch you. Do you know why?"

I shake my head and see Kenzo gripping the knife in his hand even tighter.

"Because he can't touch what's mine and I'm not sharing him with you." A finger slips through my folds and he says, "Oh, you shaved for me." I did. I stole his razor—I internally giggle—and he'll find out when he goes to use it again. "But you left me a strip. I like it." He hums, and I feel him move even closer.

"Start stroking him, love, and don't freak out."

Kyson hasn't spoken to me like this before. It's hot, and I don't know what to say or do about it. So I start moving my hand up and down Kenzo's shaft.

I hear the sound of a wrapper, and I don't dare move. I'm still on my knees but bent over now. Kenzo raises his knife, which is small but enough to slice a decent cut if he wants to. I watch as he licks his lips while my hand moves over him, and his knife finds his skin. He cuts himself right on the groin area near his penis, and a small trickle of blood appears. There is no doubt he is fascinated by it.

Kyson's fingers move to my entrance, and he inserts one inside me.

"So wet," Kyson murmurs. "What's our safe word?"

I look up to Kenzo as I say it, "Madness."

For some reason, Kenzo's eyes seem to glisten, and my hand grips his cock even tighter.

I feel Kyson move, dropping to his knees, and as I take a breath, Kyson slides into me, and I stop all movement. My body locks tight, and he reaches between my legs and touches my clit, applying the perfect amount of pressure. He must feel the moment I start to relax because he removes his hand and starts thrusting. My eyes close, but I remember to move my hand, which is still gripped around Kenzo's cock.

"Let me touch her," Kenzo says.

"No."

"But you let me touch all the others," Kenzo argues.

"Not this one."

I open my eyes to see a spark of something in Kenzo's. He cuts himself again, and I don't even bother looking at the blood as it drips right near my hand.

Kyson's thrusts pick up speed, and he grunts. One hand gently slides up my back until it reaches my hair. He clutches a handful by the roots and pulls hard, taking over full control. Using my hair, he tugs me up, still thrusting into me, not slowing his movements, as he holds me against him.

I let go of Kenzo's dick to put both hands on my head, hoping to God Kyson doesn't pull my hair out, but when he pushes into me deeper and grunts, my hands fly to my breasts and I squeeze them.

"Fuck, let me taste her...just once."

I whimper at the desperation in Kenzo's voice.

"*No*. Now leave," Kyson orders him.

Frustrated, Kenzo stands, his cock right in line with my face, and I moan. Kyson pulls my hair again, and I open my mouth to scream, but Kyson growls, "Shut it."

I do as he commands and lose sight of Kenzo.

Kyson slaps me hard, right across my breasts, before he does the same to my pussy. Then he lifts a finger and places it to my mouth. "Suck," he says.

This man has been yanking on my hair the whole time.

I'm totally going to have a headache after this.

But, fuck, it's so worth it.

As soon as I suck and wet his finger, he pulls it away and moves it to my clit where he rubs circles against the hard nub. And before I know it, I'm coming, hard.

"See, love...you didn't need him. You only wanted the idea of him." Kyson lets go of my hair, pulls out of me, and stands, leaving me on my knees. He moves in front of me, throwing the condom to the side, and nods to his hard cock. "Now, suck." I open my mouth and take him in as far as I can. I suck him so hard I gag and think I might vomit. But luckily, I don't. After he comes down my throat, he pulls out, his cock shiny and still semi-hard, then he smirks and touches my chin. "What a perfect little slut."

SEVENTEEN

Kyson

KALILAH PUSHES AWAY FROM ME, and the glare she gives me would strike me dead if she had the power to do that.

"How dare you," she seethes. "You...think, you think I'm...for fuck's sake!"

She can't even say the word as if it tastes bitter on her tongue.

"I don't actually think you're a slut, Kalilah." I try to reason with her.

The only problem is her face has gone red, her chin high, and her eyes protrude as anger radiates from her.

"Th-that..." she stutters, unable to form words. "Fuck. You!" Kalilah storms off, and I have to hold back my chuckle as she stomps past me with her red ass and her blue-black back.

Quickly, I jump up and follow her, grabbing hold before she can walk into her room. Then I spin her around. "Women like to be degraded during sex… It's a damn turn-on," I explain.

I see the tears building in her eyes, and I don't know if I have ever seen her cry and it hits me hard.

What is she doing to me?

I wouldn't even share her with my brother, which is so foreign to me. I had no problem sharing Lilly with him and anyone before her, but Kalilah is different.

Why? I have no idea.

She swipes angrily at her eyes. "Don't say that to me *ever* again. I don't like it."

Promptly, I lean in and wipe under her eyes with my thumbs and lock my gaze with hers. "I don't think of you like that. I think you are amazing."

Her eyes go wide at my words, and she whispers, "Thank you," but she pulls away. Kalilah takes a few steps, stops but doesn't turn around, and says, "I need help washing my back. Would you?"

I nod even though she can't see me and follow her to the bathroom. She turns the faucets for the shower and steps in. I trail close behind and step in under the hot water.

"I've never done anything like that before," she admits, and I reach for the soap and start to gently wash her back.

"Did you enjoy it?" I ask.

She leans into my touch.

"Yes. Is that bad?" She looks over her shoulder at me with her haunted eyes.

"No. Pleasure is never something to be ashamed of. You should embrace it," I tell her. "But I won't be doing that again."

She looks away and nods her head. "You did it with her, right?" she asks.

"I did," I say. "Lilly loved the pain. She loved to be watched and admired by more than one man. I'm amazed she's married, to be honest."

Lilly's a masochist and enjoyed having more than one partner at the same time, and I liked it. She was easy to share, and I never got jealous. I'm not really sure why, nor do I think I even want to understand the why of it.

"She doesn't love him, just so you're aware. The way she was looking at you, it's not her husband she loves," she says.

"I don't love her. I never did. She was just there,

filling up unused space which she tried to live in. When I broke it off with her, she went crazy. Told me I would come back to her and that she knew better.

"When I didn't return to her after the first month, she showed up begging me to take her back. I told her no, but Lilly returned again and again. Until one day, she stopped showing up. Not long after, I got an invite to her wedding. I contemplated not going, but in the end, I'm glad I did. Not only so I knew for sure I was over her, but because that's where I met you."

She turns around to face me with a smile on her lips. "Let's not forget you basically told me I had to come with you or I'd be dead."

"It was the truth." I shrug.

Kalilah smirks and rubs her hands over the soap before she starts washing me. My cock twitches at her touch, and her hand slides lower to cup my balls and then she grabs hold of my dick. "You make me so tired," she mumbles.

"In the best possible way."

She nods but doesn't loosen her grip as she strokes me slowly. I should tell her to stop. But I can't. My hands frame her face, and before I know it, my lips are on hers. I kiss her, and she kisses me back, opening her mouth so I have full access. My hands thread through her hair, and this time I don't pull. I hold on for dear life though, and wonder what the fuck this tiny woman is doing to me.

And, more importantly, how can I make it stop?

"She's asleep." I turn to see Kenzo at my bedroom door, looking like he hardly slept at all.

"And it looks like you haven't slept at all," I reply.

Kenzo scrubs his hand down his face, and I forget how fucked-up he is. How his soul yearns for something more sinister. "I haven't been sleeping…" he pauses, "much."

I pull Kalilah closer to me, and she molds herself to my body tighter. "Get in bed," I tell him.

As kids, it's all we knew. As we got older, we outgrew a lot of things, but some things remained, like playing with women together. Now, I'm not too keen on sharing. It's a different bond when you are a twin and unlike anything you can explain. I know how he feels, even when he doesn't want to voice it.

"I just came…" He trails off and looks past me.

"Get in," I tell him again, not really wanting to repeat myself.

Kenzo walks around to Kalilah's side of the bed. He doesn't lift the sheets but climbs on next to her. I tuck her under my arm, then look over to see him staring at the ceiling.

"She's good for you," Kenzo mumbles as he side-eyes her and then adds, "I like her."

Kenzo rarely likes anyone, so it's rare for him to even say that.

"Better than Lilly?" I ask, knowing his hatred for her. His nose scrunches as if he's eaten something bitter, and he looks back to the ceiling.

"No contest, but she snores. Should we teach her how we stop snoring?" I smile at his question. We found Zuko passed out once when he was a teenager, snoring. We held his nose until he woke up screaming and kicking. He kicked our asses, but it was so worth it at the time.

"No, I have no problem with her snoring. It's so soft and just her…" I trail off.

He nods, then turns his back to us and starts breathing more deeply.

He's passed out.

Good.

EIGHTEEN

Kalilah

I WAKE WRAPPED IN HEAT.

Oh my God! I try to move, to shift so the heat will dissipate, but it doesn't.

"Stop fucking moving." I hear Kyson grumble next to me. He holds me around my waist with his head on my shoulder.

"It's too hot. I'm suffocating," I groan, trying to get away from him.

"Stay still."

I freeze.

That was not *Kyson.*

"Most can't tell our voices apart. It amuses me that you can," Kyson says.

"Don't be." I push up between them. Once I'm on my knees, I turn, and they're both lying there.

What the hell! I was dead in the middle. Shaking my head, I climb to the end of the bed and get off. I am wearing no clothes, so I reach for Kyson's shirt on the floor.

"That isn't mine. Drop it." I do as Kyson says, turning and heading to the bathroom, where I know his clothes will be neatly tossed in a hamper. I'm starting to think he may have a cleaning problem.

I pick up a shirt, lift it over my head, and throw it on before walking back into the bedroom. Both of them are lying on their backs, their heads to the side, sound asleep.

I stand there for a minute, watching them.

They're both as beautiful as each other, one bare and tanned, the other covered in ink. The brothers are completely different, yet both the same. I grin as they both fidget at the exact same time. I wonder if they know they even sleep the same. Still grinning, I head to my room.

Nancy pales when she sees me, then calms down. "Good, good! Please tell her to leave. She won't listen to me." She grips my hand and starts pulling me. For a little old lady, she sure is strong. Nancy tugs me down the stairs, and that's when I see her. *Lilly.* Her eyes are wet, but there is no doubt

159

the tears are fake. As soon as she sees me, her back straightens, and her eyes narrow.

"You," she seethes.

Nancy stays next to me, holding my hand.

"See, he's asleep. Please leave," Nancy says.

"It's early. He should be awake. He's always awake this early," Lilly says, crossing her arms over her chest.

"Sorry, he's not. I tired him out." I wave to the door. "You can leave now."

She flicks her blonde hair behind her ear before her eyes narrow at me. "He will tire of you."

"Like he tired of you?" I bite back.

Nancy gives my hand a small squeeze.

"He never did. He just couldn't give me what I wanted. And I knew what I wanted."

"You want him. It's obvious," I say. "Even Nancy here knows the truth."

"It's best you go, Miss Lilly. Mr. Hunter does not like unwelcomed guests."

The bitch has the audacity to point her finger at me. "*She* is unwelcome."

"I'm getting really tired of this. You either leave, or I'll kick you in the cunt to get you out. You pick." I pull my hand away from Nancy and cross my arms over my chest.

"You wouldn't." She scoffs.

"Oh, but she would!" We all turn to *that* voice. Kyson walks down the stairs in only a pair of boxers. "Lilly, why are you here?"

"We need to talk. *Now*." She looks over her shoulder at me. "Alone."

I scrunch up my nose before I hear Kyson's reply. "Nancy, take Kalilah into the kitchen, I need to talk to Lilly."

Oh my God, no he did not. I glare daggers at the back of his head.

"Kalilah, if you think about hitting me…"

I poke my tongue out at him and turn around to go up the stairs. Kenzo is standing a few steps behind me, pulling his shirt on. *How did I not hear him enter the room?* He reaches out and grips me by the waist to stop me from going any farther.

"Hold up, what's the rush?" He eyes me before glancing over my shoulder, and that's when he sees Lilly. "I see the trash brought itself in."

"Fuck you! You are a sick fuck, Kenzo!" Lilly shouts.

I turn back and see Kyson watching us. His eyes are zeroed in on where Kenzo's hand is now on the middle of my back.

I turn back to Kenzo and say, "I'm coming with

you. I have the day off, and I don't want to be around them."

"Them?" he asks before it clicks. "*Ohhh.*" He nods, and I run off to quickly grab a skirt, pulling it on before I snatch up my purse and run back out to Kenzo, who is still waiting for me.

"Shit. You move fast." He chuckles.

"You gotta when you don't want to be around what the dog brought in."

His lip twitches at my words, but he doesn't laugh or even smile. "Fair enough."

"Kenzo," Kyson warns as we walk toward the door. I reach for my shoes as Kyson approaches us. "She isn't permitted to leave."

I turn around and stick my tongue out at him again.

"I'll bite it off," Kyson growls.

Lilly steps forward to touch his shoulder, but he shrugs her off like her touch means nothing. Kenzo steps out the door, and I go to follow, but Kyson grabs my hand.

"I wouldn't go far," he says in a low tone.

I look to Lilly while Kyson has a hold of me. "You can have him," I tell her.

Kyson goes to pull me back, but I manage to slip from his grip and hurry out before he can grab me again. When I get outside, I see a motorcycle in the driveway. Kenzo holds out a helmet, and I remember I'm in a skirt.

Fuck it!

Running over, I grab it, put it on, and climb onto the bike. I swear I hear Kenzo chuckle, but I can't be sure. As he pulls onto the street, I glance back to see Kyson standing there, and he's furious.

"Where are we?" I ask.

"It's a club," he replies.

"What type of club?" Looking at the building, it doesn't have any signs or give any clues, and there don't seem to be people coming and going.

"A sex club." I stop in my tracks, and Kenzo keeps walking. As he steps up to the door, it swings open, and a man is standing there. They seem friendly, greeting each other with a handshake and a smile. Then they both turn their attention to me.

"You can come in with me. I have to collect some shit," Kenzo says.

The door opens again, and a woman pops out. She has her two-toned hair—blonde on top and brown tips below—tied back, and she looks at the men before her eyes shift to mine before she says, "You bring company for a change, Kenzo?" Then she addresses me, "Come in, come in." She waves me over, and I look to Kenzo, who nods. I step toward her as she holds the door open. "Kenzo never brings anyone but his brothers," she says, letting me enter ahead of her.

"Is this really a sex club? I ask her.

"Yup. One that specializes in desires." She winks. "I'm Avani, and you don't look like the type who likes blood play." Her eyes run up and down me. "I run this place. Grayson, the man talking to Kenzo, is the boss. Well, he pays for everything. I'm really the boss around here." She chuckles, and her eyes light with mischief.

"Definitely *not* into blood," I reply.

"Yeah, didn't think so." She eyes me again. "We aren't open, but I can show you around." I shake my head. "You aren't interested in the red room?" she questions.

"Red room?" She points to a red ribbon on the counter.

"Colors for each room. Red is the blood room… Kenzo's favorite," she explains.

"Yeah, I can see that," I say.

Avani looks at me like she wants to say more but doesn't.

"I'm Kalilah. I'm staying with Kyson."

"That makes more sense. I can see you with Kyson." She glances to the door where Kenzo is standing and still in conversation with the owner of the club.

"What do you mean by that?" I ask.

She leans over and grabs my wrist, turns it over, and puts it back down. "No cuts."

"Yeah, like I said, I'm not into blood play, but I've seen ways to hide the evidence of it," I reply, remembering how Kenzo cut himself near his groin.

"I'd bet my designer bag collection I know exactly whose hidden cuts you have seen." She wiggles her brows. "I'd heard stories the Hunter twins like to share. Gosh, I'd love to know more." Avani leans in like I'm about to give her all the dirty details.

"Avani," someone growls, and I turn to Grayson. He has several tattoos—not like Kenzo, who is almost covered in ink—but Grayson's are more spaced out.

"I was being nice," Avani says.

"Yeah, you don't know how to be."

She rolls her eyes.

"It's time to go," Kenzo says, sliding something into his pocket.

"You don't want to show me the red room?" I ask.

Everyone goes deathly silent.

Kenzo's eyes flare at my question, but he remains quiet like he isn't sure what to say, but I can see the lust that sneaks into his eyes at my words.

Then someone's phone starts buzzing, and we all look at Kenzo.

"Only four people have my number. One of them is standing here. Any guess who this is?" Kenzo says, reaching into his pocket and pulling out his phone. His brother's name flashes on the screen, and he passes it to me. I take it and scrunch my nose, then close my eyes and sigh.

"Trouble in paradise?" Avani asks.

"Avani," Grayson growls.

Why do I get the feeling he has to rein her in—like a lot?

"Answer it. He'll already be pissed," Kenzo adds.

Dammit! I put the phone to my ear, and Kyson's voice demands from the other end, "Bring. Her. Back."

"Why?" I ask. There are three sets of eyes

watching me intently. Most likely, they can hear everything Kyson is saying because he's loud.

"Where are you? I'll come get you myself," Kyson barks.

"No. I got paid and need clothes. Kenzo will drop me off at the stores." I hang up and hand the phone back to Kenzo.

"I'm not going shopping with you," Kenzo says, with no care in the world.

"I know. I never said you were. I just need a ride." I smile, pulling my bag higher on my shoulder. "Plus, I need one of those now I have a job." I point to his phone is in his hand. He nods, and we say our goodbyes as we walk out. Kenzo hands me the helmet and turns to look at me before he puts his on.

"You're mad at him?" he asks.

"Yes…no… I don't know." I shrug.

"He doesn't want her. He'd still have her if he did. He kicked her to the curb long ago," he says and mounts the bike.

I let his words sink in.

Even if Kyson doesn't want her, it still pissed me off that he dismissed me like I was some kind of intruder, and now he's being all possessive and demanding I come back.

I mean, *what the actual?*

Hugging Kenzo a little closer, he speeds up, and it isn't long before he drops me off in front of a line of stores without a word, and I watch as he drives off.

I need to shop.

How exciting.

NINETEEN

Kyson

"YOU NEED TO LEAVE," I tell Lilly, turning away from her, my phone still in my hand. It dings, and it's my brother telling me where he left Kalilah.

"I've left him for you. We can try again. I won't ask for as mu—" I stop at her words with my hand and shake my head as I turn around to face her.

"Did I ask you to do that?" I step closer, and she checks my phone in my hand. "Did I?"

"Well, no. But we had so much fun together," she whispers.

"*Had* being the operative word," I say. "You can leave now. And don't come back." Turning, I place my hand on the railing as she speaks again, "You'll just use her the same way you used me. It's what you do, Kyson."

"And yet you keep coming back." I smile, turning around to face her. "You got yourself a husband, and here you stand…" I wave in front of myself.

"I hate you, Kyson."

"So why are you here?" I question. "Oh, he doesn't know how to fuck you right, does he?" I smirk, walking back down the stairs toward her. She sucks in a breath when I get close. "He doesn't know how much you like to play with more than one person." I lick my lips, and she mimics the action. "Or how you liked to be spanked."

"I—"

"You're already out of breath, Lilly. Maybe you should focus more of your energy on teaching your husband how to fuck you." I lift my hand, and she thinks I'm going to touch her, but I point behind her. "Now *fucking* leave." I turn and stride off.

"Nancy, if she doesn't go, you have my permission to stab her. We will deal with the ramifications," I call out.

"Okay, Mr. Hunter," Nancy says as I take the stairs two at a time.

Quickly, I get dressed, make my bed, and grab my keys.

A hunting we will go, a hunting we will go…

Finally, I have someone to hunt.

And we all know how much I *love* hunting.

I need to satiate my urges.

The fantastic notion of this hunt?

I already know where she is…

I'm not sure how I miss her, but now that I see her, it registers straight away. She has a slight sway to her hips that makes me bite my lip, thinking about those handprints I left on her ass.

Perhaps she is too perfect for me.

That woman's gotten me out of my head, and she's done it so damn easy. Kalilah's taking up room in there where it was once filled with *what ifs* and *what the fuck am I doing,* and now I'm consumed with when and where I can touch her next.

I stand back and observe. Kalilah leans down to pick up a skirt. She's oblivious to everyone around her, in her own little world. A sales assistant approaches to offer her a hand. Kalilah smiles and clearly tells them no. Her hands are full of bags, and I stand here, just a little longer, admiring the incredible view.

I come up behind her while she's still bent over

and looking at something the bottom rack, trying to find the correct size.

"I'd prefer you naked," I whisper.

Kalilah jumps at my voice, hitting me in the stomach as she does. She sucks in a breath, places a hand over her heart, and turns around to face me with those golden eyes filled with anger.

"Did you bring your little friend?" she asks, scanning the area. "You did tell me to leave so you two could talk. So why are you here?" Kalilah bites out, clearly pissed.

"I thought I would let her down gently."

"Oh, cause she clearly deserves that. How nice of you." She gives me an eye roll before she turns and stomps off.

"She does. Lilly seeing you staying with me would have been a blow to her. She never slept over," I try to explain.

"I don't see how that's *my* problem." Kalilah reaches down on another rack and picks up a skirt. "Now, if you could leave, I was having a good day shopping."

"You can't afford all that," I say, nodding to the pile of clothes she has in her hands.

"Well, I do know that. But thanks for shouting it out for everyone to hear, you asshole."

I take the pile from her arms and walk over to the register. "All of it," I tell the woman manning the counter.

"I can pay for my own shit." Kalilah tries to nudge me out of the way with her hip, but I don't go anywhere. I tap my card before she can even reach for hers and smile at the sales assistant, who is eyeing us with a soft look.

Kalilah turns and storms out without even grabbing her bags.

I swipe them off the counter and hurry out after her, following her into a cell phone store.

"You need a phone?" I ask.

"Yes. I gave work a fake number. They said they tried to call, and a man answered. So I need one so I can tell them the right number before they figure out I lied and lose my damn job."

A sales assistant starts running through the phone options with Kalilah. She seems confused as to what to get. It's as if she hasn't owned one in an incredibly long time which is strange.

"We'll take that one." I point to the newest one —a touch screen that should be easy for her to use. It's the same one I have. When the sales assistant walks away, Kalilah side-eyes me.

"I can't afford that one," she whispers, embarrassed.

"I can," I reply, heading to the counter and paying for it.

When I'm done, I walk back to find her exactly where I left her. She seems lost in thought like she can't work anything out that's happening around her. Her golden eyes are shining, and she shakes her head when I repeat her name a few times and then ask, "What's wrong?"

Kalilah turns and walks out of the store.

Now I'm left carrying three of her bags.

She stops at a bench and sits down, leans forward, and places her head in her hands.

I take a seat cautiously next to her. "Do you need instructions to breathe? Because I'm going to be honest, I'm usually the one to stop someone breathing, not show them how."

She turns her head in her hands and looks at me with a soft smile touching her lips.

"What's wrong?" I repeat.

"It makes me uncomfortable that you do that." She waves her hand to the material possessions in the bags.

"Why? Women love gifts."

"Is that what those are…gifts? Or entrapment?" she whispers.

"No, they're gifts," I say, confused.

"The last man who bought me gifts," she uses air quotes, "took them away just as quickly."

"The husband," I state, and Kalilah nods.

"I haven't had a phone since we were married. He took that as well."

"How did you get by?"

"What do you mean? With him or the phone? I didn't need a phone because I never went anywhere or had any friends. As for him, I did everything for him," she says like it's obvious. "And now this," she waves her hands around the bags, "makes me uncomfortable."

"Okay. You can come and clean my room as payment." Before she can say anything, I hold up a finger and add, "Naked, preferably."

"Your room is already clean. You're a clean freak," she says.

Yes, that is true. There's no denying it.

"Okay, point taken. But you could do something else naked." I wiggle my brows at her.

"If I take those from you…" she motions to the things in my hands yet again, "you are to never ask for them back or remind me you paid for them. Especially considering I never asked you to," she says seriously. So seriously, she crosses her arms over her chest and inhales deeply, trying to get the point across to me.

"I didn't buy them to bribe you, Kalilah. Fuck! How fucked-up was your husband?"

"Okay, I'll take them. But please don't do that again unless I ask."

"You won't ask," I argue.

Kalilah nods again, this time, smiling. "See, you're learning." She stands and looks down at me. "I'm also going to be looking for a place to live soon. I don't want to stay with you forever."

I stand at her words.

Nope, not happening!

"Why?" I ask.

"Because I want to be free. And right now, you won't allow that."

"I will," I insist, and she eyes me suspiciously.

"Okay. We'll see."

We will.

I hope.

TWENTY

Kalilah

_____

SOMEHOW, I keep ending up in his bed, even when I go to sleep in my own. It's been almost two weeks, and I have managed to save my paycheck, apart from the first. It's easy when you don't have to pay for food or gas. He always has the car filled for me without me saying anything.

There have been one or two nights when I've gone to bed, and he hasn't brought me to his room, but when I wake up and go to see if he's awake, his bed is untouched, which means he never came home.

And those are my most restless nights.

He doesn't know it yet, but I've been looking for somewhere to live, and I know he won't like it, and he'll try to make me stay. But I get the feeling he'll let me go because he knows it's what I need.

I'm about to head out for the day when he walks in, his eyes tired, looking straight past me. I'm in one of his shirts, as I usually am, and a pair of shorts. I enjoy wearing his shirts, and he doesn't seem to mind all that much.

"Are you okay?" I ask him.

Kyson runs his hand through his hair, and when he raises his head and takes a step toward me, I can tell there's something different in his eyes. Something fiercer.

His boots leave footprints of blood and something else on the floor, and my bag slides down my arm as I let it go. He reaches me in two steps, slams me back into the wall, and lifts me. I'm so shocked that I simply go along with what he's doing. He tears at my clothing, trying to pull my shirt off, but it's not working. When I look into his eyes, I see anger, and I wonder if it's directed at me.

I help him and quickly pull the shirt over my head. Kyson sets me back on my feet, then with both hands, he rips at my shorts, pulling them down in one swift movement, taking my underwear with them. He lifts me, now completely naked, back into his arms, and before I can say anything, he's at my entrance and pushing in.

I've had hard and fast sex before, but this is rough and unpredictable, and my heart is beating fast, but not in a bad way. I know this man is dangerous. Fuck, he's literally tracked blood in on his boots. He's either killed someone or was there when it happened.

None of that seems to bother me right now as his hands grip my ass cheeks, squeezing them and pushing me down as far as I can go onto his cock.

"Kyson," I say his name, but he isn't registering any words leaving my mouth. The grip he has on my ass has become painful, but it's good. He moves me up and down so I'm sliding on his cock. He leans forward and bites me just above my nipple, and a small scream erupts from my lips, but he doesn't stop. And I don't ask him to because the pain and pleasure mixed together is something I didn't know I enjoyed this much until him.

He pulls his mouth away, only to come straight back and bite my other breast before his tongue circles where his teeth marks have broken the skin. He moves lower, putting my nipple in his mouth, rolling it around on his tongue before he bites that as well. I can feel the sting as my nails claw at his back, digging in as far as they can go. Then he slaps my ass as hard as humanly possible.

Holy shit.

"Fuck! I love fucking you," he growls.

I want to tell him that I enjoy it as well, but before I get a chance, he slaps my other ass cheek and pulls us away from the wall. He's now standing in the middle of the hallway, still guiding me up and down, but at this point, my feet are locked behind his back, and my hands are over his shoulders, nails digging into his skin as I push myself up and down on his cock.

One of his hands skates up my back and grips my ponytail, tipping my head back. I manage to grab the back of his neck so I don't fall, but he has no intention of letting me, his other hand is still holding me up under my ass.

I feel him take a step, but I don't know what he's doing until my upper back hits the railing. His hands are now both clamped on my hips, and I'm leaning back as he continues to fuck me. My hands run through my hair as I try to stop the scream that wants to erupt from deep in my chest.

"See, such a good girl," he croons as I come.

I reach for him, but he doesn't let me touch him as he reaches his own orgasm.

And when he's done, I look to the side and scream. "Pull me up! Oh my God, pull me up, you fuckhead!"

He chuckles and pulls me back. I didn't realize that the only thing holding me up was his grip on my hips. If he'd let me go at any point, I would have fallen to the floor below.

I claw at him until I'm standing on my own two feet, trying to calm my breathing. The white railing where he just fucked me will never look the same.

"You didn't use the safe word," he whispers.

I turn and snatch my shirt from the floor.

"I had plans, and now I have to shower," I say, not looking at him as I walk back to my room.

Kyson goes to follow me, but I shut the door behind me, and he doesn't come in.

And when I leave, he isn't there.

"So, real talk. How's the sex?" Alaska asks as we sit down at a local café. She got my number and asked me to lunch. She said she's trying this new thing where she tries to make friends, and at least I know what crazy she's involved with, so it can't be that bad.

I blush, and she waves a hand at me.

"You know I talk dirty for a living, right? Men, and even women, pay me to tell them how hot they make me over the phone," she says, flicking her lavender hair back. I wonder if her customers know they're talking to a goddess on the other side of that phone. This woman in front of me is beautiful in every conceivable way.

"It's hot. Good and rough," I admit, and she laughs.

"Honey, you don't even want to get me started on rough." She snorts as the coffee is brought over.

"Huh?" I say, confused.

She leans in close, then asks with a raised brow, "You ever come by having a knife up your vag?"

"Can't say that I have," I tell her.

"Okay, well… I have. And despite how much I wanted to kill him, he was the first man to make me come." She shrugs. "But if he thinks he can do that again, I'll use that knife and slice off a finger because, you know, I still need his cock." She cackles.

My eyes dart around the café, but I see no one's paying us any attention. Reaching for the top of my shirt, I pull it down slightly to show her.

Alaska's eyes go wide, and she sits back. "He's a biter," she states. "Are there more?"

"Nipples and other breast."

"Okay." She nods. "Anything else?"

"He likes to yank my hair and spank my ass," I whisper.

"*Ohh...* I'm so going to tease him in some way about this."

My cheeks flush. "No, please don't."

"Okay, I won't. But the real question is, do you like it?"

"Love it," I say quietly. "I don't know why. I just do. He makes me forget everything around us, and I get lost in him."

"I know that feeling well," she says, smiling.

"And..." I lick my teeth.

"There's more?" She leans in.

"If you promise to not repeat it," I say.

"I do," she replies seriously, and I believe her.

"He likes his brother to watch." Her eyes go wide. "It was only once, but it was hot."

"Holy Batman... are you joking?"

"Nope. It was a thing they did. I heard they used to share."

"I heard Kenzo likes to cut," she says.

"Yeah, he does." I flash back to him cutting himself.

"Did he cut you?" She eyes me.

"God, no." I shake my head. "It's all just a lot, you know? I went from being in a prison of a marriage to a runaway, to basically homeless, to this." I wave my hand around.

"For someone as young as you, that's a lot to take in. It makes you grow quickly. I get that part more than you can imagine." She goes quiet before she asks, "Which part did you like the most?"

"The now. I know Kyson still holds most of the control, but I like the now." I smile.

"Okay, so what's the plan? We looking for a place?" she asks.

"You don't have to come. I know you probably have other plans."

"I have one friend, who will get jealous of this, by the way, but I'm sure she'll be extremely happy I am venturing out and making new friends." She smiles, standing. "Where to first?"

I rattle off the address, and her eyes light up.

"That's right near my place. Can we stop there really quick? I want to change shoes." I look down at the wedge shoes she's wearing, and she shakes her head. "Don't even ask. I tried to dress all girly, but I want my sneakers." I laugh.

Not long after, I follow her back to her place, which isn't too far from where we'd met up.

She parks her red car and gets out, then comes over to me. "The guys are here. You want to come in and say hi?" I see Kenzo's bike and contemplate my answer. *Is Kyson here too?* I wonder.

"Come on… Won't be long." She opens my car door, and I slide out, then follow her inside. Silence fills the room when we walk in. There are three men—two I know well, the other is Alaska's partner and the twins' older brother.

He freaks me out until I see him with Alaska. His hands find hers, and he pulls her in, his whole body seeming to soften at her simple touch.

"Kalilah, fancy seeing you here," Kenzo drawls, sitting back and smirking. I glance at Kyson, who's watching me. "You don't say hi?" Kenzo says. He's lounged back in the same position as his twin brother, and I wonder if they have any idea how much alike they are.

I look at Zuko and smile, but he doesn't smile back, so mine drops.

I turn my attention to Alaska, who pushes away from Zuko before she bends down and undoes her shoes. She quickly slips them off and heads to the bedroom, leaving me with the three brothers.

"I'm going to wait outside. Can you tell Alaska?" I don't wait for an answer and head to the door.

"Are your tits okay?" Kyson asks. I stop as I reach for the door handle and glance over my shoulder at him.

"Yes," I answer.

"I can always make them better. You never used the word," he states.

"I didn't need to." I pull the door open and walk out.

Alaska's not far behind me.

TWENTY-ONE

Kyson

"WHAT WAS THAT ABOUT?" Kenzo asks as Zuko takes a seat at the table. "What did you do to her tits?"

"That isn't the issue," I reply.

"No, you going ape shit and locking up her husband is," Zuko seethes. I bite my bottom lip as I watch them. "Is he still alive?" he asks.

"For now," I say, unconcerned.

"Care to tell us where he is?" Kenzo asks.

"Nope."

"You know that's not how we work," Zuko scolds.

"I know, but this one is *mine*."

"You have strong feelings for this woman," Zuko says, surprised.

"He shouldn't have come looking for what's not his." I shrug my shoulders.

"Does she know he came looking for her?" Kenzo asks.

"No, of course not."

"You know I can track you anywhere, right?" Kenzo says, leaning in.

"If you do, I'll kick your fucking head in."

Kenzo nods and sits back.

"What do you plan to do about Pops?" Zuko asks. I filled him in on all the information I had found out about Pops. It seems we've had blankets over our eyes for many years when it comes to him.

"Nothing. That will be Kenzo's issue since he's the one who is always up his ass lately," I add, and Zuko turns to Kenzo.

"What do you plan to do?" Zuko asks.

"He made us who we are. I say we find more evidence before we decide on anything. He hasn't made any moves against us, and all we have is hearsay." Zuko and I stare at him.

"We have evidence; it's a folder full of it. He is, or at the very least planning to train others," I add. Kenzo grinds his jaw. "If he makes a move, I will kill him. But for now. It's all yours Kenzo, you can deal with him. Do you understand?"

"He wouldn't kill you." Sometimes I think he is blind to Pop's, his loyalty to him blinds him.

"I'm leaving it, for now. But make no mistake, I will kill him as easily as I breath if I hear or see anything else." Zuko gives me a slight nod and I know he agrees with me.

Kenzo and I were once inseparable, but time changes people. And now he spends more time with Pops than either of us. *I sometimes wonder if his allegiance is with Pops and not me.* But I know better than that and shut down that thought instantly.

Kenzo has always had and will always have my back.

No matter who the other person is.

Same as me with him.

I stand, not wanting to talk about Pops again. His fucked-up ways and him hiding shit from us? I'm over it. I don't plan to do any more jobs for him, and I don't plan to see him again any time soon. I know that eventually he will get pissed off and possibly react in a way that I least expect; that's the thing with Pops, you never know which way he will go. He keeps all secrets and his intentions close to him, but then again, he taught us to do the same. But right now, he is the least of my problems. I have someone locked away in my basement who had absolutely no right to step foot on my property.

The boys don't say anything when I leave.

And Kenzo will be none the wiser because the sleazebag husband is at my house, so he can't track me to where he thinks I may have him. He wouldn't think for a second I would bring him home because he knows how much I love my space and how particular I am with certain things.

Kalilah has even come to realize how I am. I'm not exactly sure what her plans were today, and a part of me doesn't care because I'm glad she's not at the house when I return. I spot Nancy straight away, cooking away in the kitchen, with soft, slow music flowing through the house. I sit at the counter as she finishes plating.

"I need you to go out tonight, Nancy. For the whole night."

She starts to speak but then sees something in my eyes and instead says, "I can do that." Nancy points to the food on the counter and then back to me. "Please eat. You need to keep your strength up for that goddamn awful human who hurt our girl." I don't ask her how she knows he's here and who he is. Nancy has been loyal for many years and has become, over those years, very observant.

She walks past me and pats my shoulder before she leaves.

"Goodnight, Nancy."

She tells me the same as she heads to the door.

I would usually lock the house, but I don't want to risk Kalilah not being able to get in. I'm not one hundred percent sure she has keys, as Nancy is usually here whenever she comes home.

Walking into the garage, I head straight to the door that leads down to the basement. It's dark. I turned all the lights off before I left. When I flick them on, his face comes into view, and he blinks rapidly against the lights. The asshole struggles against the restraints, but obviously, that doesn't get him anywhere. I want to tell him how useless it is, but I don't bother. I could tie a man up in three seconds, and if he were really good, it would still take him an hour to get loose. Trust me, my brothers and I have tried all the tricks.

"You stink." I can tell he's urinated all over himself. At my words, he looks down between his legs, where his blood is mixing with his urine.

What a despicable motherfucker.

How she ever fell in love with him is beyond my capability of understanding.

The asshole is in his mid-forties. He basically

married Kalilah as soon as she was of legal age and then trapped her. She didn't stand a chance. I did some deeper research and found that both her parents are still alive, and they often post memories of her on their Facebook accounts. Attached to these posts are messages saying they hope that one day she will come home.

I wonder what he did to get her to stop seeing her parents. I investigated their backgrounds too. They seem to be happy. She did too. It's amazing what manipulation can do to someone when you know how to use it like a weapon.

I pull the gag off his mouth and take a seat opposite him.

"You want her," he snarls. "She's married, so you can't have her." It's quite funny, considering the situation he's currently in, tied to a chair and stabbed in the leg. Yet he still thinks he has some sort of control.

I stand up, then lean down, so I'm in his face, a devilish smirk touching my lips.

"She tastes phenomenal, wouldn't you agree?" His eyes widen as he registers that she is now mine. Before he can say another word, I lift my boot and stomp on his foot. I can hear the bones break, followed by the scream, before I shove the gag back into his mouth and sit back down. Tears spring to his eyes, and I mess around on my phone while I wait for him to man up and stop being a little fucking bitch.

Opening my new favorite game, I sit and play to ease my anger. When I'm finally winning, I look up to see him spit the gag out onto the floor, his face red with anger.

"You don't know who I am," he growls.

"But I do, Mr. Carmel. I know precisely who you are. What motorcycle gang you hang with. How you fucked all different types of women and claimed the most precious one for yourself. But she got away from you, didn't she?" I state. "You see, it's me who *you* don't know. Did you think you could just track her down and not check whose house you were coming to?"

"So what, you have money. I have more than that."

What an absolute dick.

I grab his phone from the table next to me and hold it up to his face to unlock it. Finding the correct name in his contact list, I call the president of his gang, and he picks up straight away.

"You've been gone way too long," a low, angry voice raises on the line.

"You must be talking about Mr. Carmel here," I reply, making sure the phone is on speaker.

"Hobs, this man is crazy. He has me tied up!" Kalilah's husband yells.

I raise a finger to shut him up. "Hobs. Is that your name?" I say. "I believe it's really Harry, but if Hobs is what you prefer, then who am I to argue." I chuckle. The dumb shit across from me, Tony, looks at me surprised. Tony Carmel. That stupid name should have been Kalilah's first red flag.

"Who the fuck is this?" Hobs barks into the phone.

"I have your man, who thinks—" The idiot hangs up, cutting me off.

Now that wasn't nice.

He doesn't play fair.

I get up and go to leave.

"He will find you," Tony calls out to my back.

"I'm looking forward to it!"

TWENTY-TWO

Kalilah
___

ALASKA IS FUN, and after we go house hunting, she takes me for drinks with her friend Louise, who kindly informs me she once flashed Kyson her hooha. I laugh at the story. I can see why they're friends—they balance each other out nicely.

When it's time for me to go, Alaska offers to take me home, but I call an Uber instead.

She waves as the driver takes off, and not long into the drive, my phone starts dinging.

I look down to see it says my Uber has arrived.

What?

That has to be a mistake.

A delayed message?

Right?

195

Maybe I had too many drinks because I'm clearly in an Uber right now.

Lying my head back against the seat, my phone continues to ding.

I send a message through the Uber app telling them I'm in the car.

The driver replies back immediately, saying he's waiting for me.

What?

"Sir? Um... I'm sorry to bother you," I say to the man driving the car.

"Yes, Kalilah?" I freeze at his use of my name. The app doesn't have my first full name, just Kal.

As I reach for the door handle, the car pulls over and stops. I jump out as fast as I can, gripping my phone for dear life, before I start running. But my legs are slow, and my breath is gone. *Fucking alcohol.* Arms wrap around me from behind and lift me up. I kick for all I am worth, but it's no use.

"I'd stop that if I were you," a voice calls out. "Seems you have caused a lot more trouble than you are worth."

Confused, I whip my head toward the voice, sobering up as I do.

Shit! Hobs. It's the president of the MC that Tony is a member of. "You ran far, but did you think he wouldn't find you?" He steps closer and grabs my chin. "You are his favorite toy. So obedient. Until you ran." He shakes his head, his hold on my chin becoming tighter. His fingers almost bruising as he grips me. "Now, tell me where he is."

I shake my head, having no idea what he's talking about.

"I don't know, haven't seen him," I tell him. He removes his hand from my chin and uses it to slap me hard across the face. Instantly, I taste blood. Licking my lips, I meet his eyes, holding back my tears. "*I don't know*.... I'm not lying," I reply. He doesn't like my truth, so he punches me in the stomach with such force I would double over if I weren't being held up.

Talk about taking a fucking beating.

I've lost my breath and am struggling to catch it. And just when I do, he punches me again for good measure. This time, though, I spew all down my front, unable to stop myself.

"You are disgusting." He sneers at me, then addresses the person holding me. "Tie her the fuck up and check her phone."

I'm shoved to the ground, where I land on my side, my hands clutching my stomach. A moment later, my hands are yanked behind my back and tied together.

This! This was the reason I ran.

How stupid I was to get comfortable and think for even one single second I was safe.

How did I trust another man so easily when one was willing to break me down without care?

The tears break free as my phone is yanked from my hand. I lunge at the man, but he kicks me back, then scrolls through the phone. He won't find much since it's new. And I don't keep contacts. I don't even think I've messaged anyone yet, so that's a positive.

"It's empty," the man says to Hobs.

They start talking to each other, and I manage to catch my breath and scan our surroundings while they aren't looking. We're in the middle of bumfuck nowhere, but not far from here is an industrial area. I don't know it well, but someone should be there. Getting myself to my feet as quietly as I can, I take one look at them before I turn and hotfoot it the fuck out of there as fast as I can.

"Hobs!" the man shouts.

"Let her run," I hear Hobs say.

Though I'm relieved at his words, I don't slow my pace. A moment later, I hear a loud crack, and before I can even think of what the sound is, a sharp pain knocks me down. My leg feels like it's on fire, and I fall face-first to the ground, my hands still tied behind my back.

"You are *so* stupid," Hobs says before his foot nudges my leg. I turn my head toward him as he applies more pressure. I scream, and he smiles. "Run again, and the next place I shoot you will not be your leg. You're lucky it only grazed you."

I don't feel lucky.

I feel anything but lucky.

"Now, let's go find your husband." The asshole claps his hands as I'm yanked up and thrown over the other man's shoulder. The jerk carries me to the car, opens the trunk, tosses me in like trash, then shuts it. I lie there, trying to gather myself, remembering I can get out of this...

If I want it enough.

I can.

I will.

I hope.

After what feels like forever, the car starts to move, and when it eventually comes to a stop, there's absolute silence. The trunk pops open, but the darkness doesn't allow me to see who's there. I push at the person and try to kick them as they drag me out.

"Fuck this bitch," the jerk snarls.

I'm hit in the head.

Everything starts to go fuzzy, and then I'm dizzy, which gives him the opportunity to pull me from the car.

When I am finally out, that's when I see red.

A lot of red.

I follow the smeared trail to Nancy lying on the ground.

She isn't moving.

Shit!

"Nancy," I whisper shakily. I attempt to get to her, wanting to reach out, but my hands are still tied, and my leg is hurting so much that the second I put pressure on it, more tears spring to my already leaking eyes.

"She was a tough old nut. The bitch wouldn't give us any information," Hobs says with a hint of respect in his tone.

And then I realize where we are.

We're at Kyson's, in his driveway.

Does he know we're here?

Does he know Nancy is dead in his driveway?

"Call him and tell him you're here." Hob's

holds out my phone, but I can't take my gaze off Nancy because her eyes are open and blank.

Oh God, I hope she didn't suffer.

Hobs looks at the jerk with him. "Untie her hands." The other guy does as Hobs orders. As soon as my hand is free, he grips the back of my shirt—Kyson's shirt—and holds me in place.

"Take the phone, Kalilah, and don't fuck around."

I look away from Nancy.

Poor Nancy.

Wiping at my tears, I reach for the phone.

And as I do, Hobs grips my wrist.

"Careful what you say. You don't want to end up like this old lady now, do you?" He nods to Nancy before he removes his hand from my wrist. I pull the phone closer and unlock it. Kyson showed me how to use it and made me memorize his number. I have no numbers stored due to my worries about this type of situation happening.

I type in his number and press call.

Kyson answers on the first ring. "Kalilah," he breathes out. "Where are you?"

Hobs takes my phone and puts it on speaker. "Tell him where you are," Hobs says, loud enough for Kyson to hear.

"I'm out front," I whisper.

The phone goes dead instantly.

Hobs pulls me directly in front of him—*the damn coward*—as we face the door. I watch as it swings open, Kyson standing there in only a pair of jeans which are hanging low on his hips. His eyes land on me first before they scan the surrounding area. It's then he sees Nancy. His nostrils flare before his gaze comes back to me.

"Where is he?" Hobs demands.

Kyson walks down the stairs slowly. They don't think he's a threat because he looks harmless with nowhere to hide a weapon.

That is one hundred percent a mistake on their part.

"Where is he?" Hobs shouts.

"He is about to be dead, thanks to you," Kyson says calmly, eyes locked on Hobs behind me. "And if you don't care to join him, I would suggest you remove your hands from Kalilah." He stops just out of reach from me.

Hobs scoffs. "You must think I'm stupid. Do you not know who I am?"

"And you mustn't have done your research to see whose house you just rolled up to." Kyson stands there relaxed as if this is all nothing to him.

"Nice to meet you. I'm Kyson..." he pauses. "Kyson Hunter."

"I couldn't care less," Hobs sneers.

"You may have heard of me. I have two brothers, who, I might add, are pulling up right now." A car comes up the driveway, but Hobs keeps his hold on me. "Ring any bells?"

"Prez." The dude who tied me up steps closer. "We should fuckin' leave."

Hobs grips me harder.

The asshole's angry now.

"We aren't going anywhere until we have Tony."

"Prez, these are the Hunter brothers." It takes a moment to register in Hobs's brain, but when it does, he loosens his grip on me, but not enough to let me go.

I hear a car door and know who it is.

Kyson looks to his brothers and says, "Please go to the basement, grab my guest, and bring him out here." They both walk past us inside. "I'd suggest you let her go. I'm already furious you have the audacity to hurt something that's *mine*."

Hobs's breathing seems to change, and his grip loosens even more, but he still doesn't let me go. The jerk, the man he came with, on the other hand, looks around nervously, eyes scattering everywhere. He licks his lips as he looks to Hobs then to me and shakes his head before he turns, walks quickly to the car, and drives off, leaving Hobs standing there with no backup.

"Where are you hurt?" Kyson asks me.

I hold back the tears. "My leg. Where he shot me hurts the worst," I tell him. His nostrils flare at my words. "But the punches took the breath right out of me." I feel Hobs tense behind me.

"You hit her? Shot her?" Kyson snarls, his face a mask of fury. "Why the fuck would you shoot her?"

Before Hobs can answer, I hear *his* screaming.

"*You!*" he seethes. And when I turn my head, I see my husband's eyes locked on me. "All of this is because of *you*." He is limping, and I look back to Kyson.

How long has he had him?

And was he in the house the whole time?

"He's only been here for a couple of days. Don't worry, love," Kyson says as if he can read my thoughts.

"You're fucking him, you slut!" Tony screams at me. "Cut the bitch, Hobs. Remind her who her husband is."

Hobs does nothing, his arms still around me,

but his grip is much looser. "If I release her, you can have him, and I will leave." Hob's tries to bargain. "We didn't know. I didn't know," he repeats.

"What are you talking about? Cut the fucking bitch!" Tony yells.

Zuko and Kenzo seem to be bored with the situation, holding Tony between them as if it's nothing.

"If he doesn't shut up, I *will* kill him," Kenzo says, loud enough for all of us to hear.

"Shut up, Tony. You've already fucked everything up," Hobs says and looks back to Kyson.

"Do we have a deal?"

"That I can have them both?" Kyson asks.

Hobs nods.

And I know without even saying anything what a mistake that is. He steps back, hands dropping away from me.

"They are the Hunters, Tony. You're on your own with them." Hobs no longer has a car, so he turns and runs. I watch as Kyson looks back at Kenzo, who pulls out his gun.

"Just the leg," Kyson instructs, and Kenzo shoots. He doesn't even need to aim, and I am floored when he hits the intended target exactly where he needs to.

I watch as Hobs falls to the ground.

Kyson rushes over to me and kisses the top of my head. "I'm sorry, love. So sorry." He stalks past me and makes his way to Hobs, but he stops on the way, leans down, and closes Nancy's eyes, softly touching her before he gets back up and keeps walking.

Hobs tries to plead with him, but Kyson shuts him up with a few words. "I *can* have them, *you* are correct..." Kyson pauses. "But you hurt what's mine and killed a friend." He leans down and kisses the top of Hobs's head, stands tall, and smiles at him. "Goodnight." And then his foot lifts, and he brings it down, hard, stomping on Hobs's head. I look away as the sounds echo through the night, my body tensing and hurting with each stomp.

"Kalilah," Kenzo says as I fall to the ground, unable to stand any longer, and pass out...cold.

TWENTY-THREE

Kyson

DAMMIT!

I didn't expect to have Kalilah break on me again, but here she is.

Passed out as I fix her leg.

My brothers took the husband back down to the basement as I carried her inside.

"What do you want us to do about Nancy?" Kenzo asks as he stands in the doorway.

Zuko walks in and studies Kalilah.

"Check her stomach," he says, not making a move to touch her. I lift her shirt and see bruises already starting to form on her torso. Fuck! This woman has taken so many beatings I'm amazed at her strength and veracity. *Does she realize how strong she actually is?* Not only physically but mentally as well. Her husband is no prize and was lucky to have her, but he never treated Kalilah with the respect she deserves.

Turning around, I say to Kenzo, "Wrap Nancy carefully. I want to bury her."

He nods.

We don't usually bury our dead. We have other easier and safer ways of body disposal, but this is a different situation. Nancy was a good soul. Even when she was free from her husband's clutches, she still found a way to please other people. I'm not sure if I'll ever replace her. I didn't even really hire her in the first place. She kind of forced herself into the job and wouldn't take no for an answer. And to be honest, I'm glad she did because she was a wonderful addition to my life.

"She is going to be in pain," Zuko says, talking about Kalilah. "I'll call the doctor." He heads out the door without another word, and I know where he's going—back to Alaska's.

Kalilah's breathing is soft, and I wonder if she can feel pain right now. I go into the bathroom and grab a small hand towel, then take it out to wrap it around her leg. There is blood all over my bed sheets, both fresh as well as dry. She groans, and I reach for her hand as she slowly starts to stir.

"Stay calm, okay," I say, and her golden eyes find mine.

"It really hurts," she whispers.

I wipe her hair from her face. "I know, but the doctor needs to check you before I can give you anything."

"Alcohol," she grumbles.

I chuckle and shake my head. "That will thin your blood, and we can't have that," I scold gently.

She moves to get comfortable and flinches as she does.

"He did a number on your stomach," I say with venom in my voice. I can't help the anger radiating from me. She reaches for my hand, and my eyes find hers.

"I'm still alive." She smiles.

Fuck! That smile. It hits me right in the stomach every single time, making that fucker flutter.

Her mouth is smeared with dried blood, and her nose looks like it also took a beating. But I don't say anything because she's still as beautiful as ever to me.

"I didn't mean to cause you all this trouble." Her eyes go wide as she remembers and says, "And Nancy?" Her hands lift and cover her face. "Oh

God, Nancy. I'm so sorry." She starts to cry, and I stand, not sure what to do.

"She was a tough old woman. I'm sure she would have been happy to leave this life defending you. She liked you more than me," I tell her.

"I'm going to get you some ice. Stay here, okay?"

She nods, wiping away her tears.

While I'm in the kitchen, Kenzo walks in, wiping his hands on his trousers. I hear a van drive up and know it's the clean-up crew.

"Why are you down here?" he asks.

"Ice," I reply, opening the freezer where there are prepared meals frozen for me.

Fuck. That sucks. *Fuck! Nancy.*

"She was a good woman. Lord knows why she stuck around you as long as she did." I want to say it's because I paid her well, but I don't think it was the money that kept her here. She was simply loyal and wanted to do what she wanted, and that was to help me. "Would you like me to check Kalilah since you're avoiding her?" Kenzo makes to go that way, but I stop him.

"No, stay and wait for the fucking doctor."

He chuckles, knowing exactly what he's doing as I walk past him and straight up the stairs and into my bedroom. I find her trying to sit up, but she grabs her stomach, clearly forgetting she was punched several times.

"Stop moving and lie down."

Kalilah does as I say without a fight. I walk over and wrap the ice pack so it doesn't freeze her skin, and then place it on her stomach.

"Do I make you uncomfortable?" she asks. "I didn't mean to bring all this here. I tried to tell you to let me go, but you wouldn't listen."

"No, because *you* are *mine*. Why would I let you go?" I say the words without even thinking. Her brows raise, and she gets this weird look on her face like she isn't sure if she likes what I said but kind of does. I'm starting to read her better.

"I'm no one's," she whispers.

"You aren't his, but you are *mine*, Kalilah. The thing is, though, I won't trap you." I pause. "Only when you like it." I wink.

"But you did trap me," she says, shaking her head. "You made me come here, and you locked me in that room."

"I couldn't have you living in that shitbag motel anymore, and you were too stubborn to accept help. Besides, if I was trying to trap you, would I have let you use my car?"

"I don't want to belong to anyone."

A knock comes on the door, and I turn to see the doctor and Kenzo. The expression on Kenzo's face tells me he heard everything.

"Would you all mind giving us some space to work on the young lady, please," the doctor says. He has been with us for many years and is incredibly loyal. He pats my shoulder as I pass him on my way out of the room. "Shut the door, please." Kalilah's eyes stay locked on me as I do as the doctor asks. When I'm in the hallway with the door closed behind me, I see Kenzo standing there staring at me.

"You're in love," he says, a smirk teasing his lips.

"I am not," I grumble.

"You are." He chuckles and heads downstairs. I follow him all the way to the basement door.

"Do we kill him now, or…" he inquires.

"Later." I smile cruelly.

The worst thing about death is you know it's coming, but not when.

That asshole will not know.

And every time we go in to see him, he will think, *Is this the time I die?*

Not today, asshole.

You have some hell to pay first.

TWENTY-FOUR

Kalilah

THE DOCTOR CHECKS me over and tells me he
doesn't think anything is broken, just badly bruised,
then he sticks me with a needle and injects me with
some meds. I want to laugh at him because it feels
like my whole body is broken.

He is kind as he works, putting me at ease when
he tells me about his family. Doc mentions how his
wife gets shitty every time he leaves in the middle of
the night. But he just shrugs his shoulders and
smiles as he talks about her. You can tell he loves
her. He proceeds to tell me about his child, who
once went down an incredibly dangerous path, and
the only people to bring him back were the
Hunters. It's why he's indebted to them for the rest
of his life. But he says it with a smile, like it's no

issue at all, being called in the middle of the night to come and fix up some strange woman. I guess when your son completely turns his life around to become a lawyer, thanks to the Hunter brothers, nothing is too much trouble.

When he's completed his examination, I feel a little better. The drugs are finally kicking in, and my leg is stitched up. He told me to keep ice on my stomach and lip and that my stomach was going to cause me a lot of pain in the coming days.

When the doctor gets up to leave, Kyson is there. He looks to have showered and has changed clothes.

My eyes are becoming heavy, but the doctor turns back to look at me.

"It was lovely meeting you," he says. The only thing I can do is give him a small smile as my eyes start to close. He turns to Kyson. "I want you to bring her in, possibly a few weeks, no later than a month. I would like to run a few more tests, make sure everything is doing okay." I pop one eye open as Kyson nods. "I'll come back in two weeks and grab some bloodwork to ensure she has no infections."

I hear him leave and then feel the bed dip. I

want to turn on my side and curl up into a ball, but my body won't allow it.

"Sleep," Kyson says.

And with that one word, I fall fast asleep with him right next to me.

The pain is a lot to take.

I flinch when I wake up for the bathroom. I feel Kyson jump next to me, half asleep himself. I was trying not to wake him as I got up, but I've obviously failed. The meds have worn off, and it hurts. And my bladder is letting me know in no uncertain terms I need to relieve myself.

"Fuck. Just wait, would ya." Kyson gets up, naked, and comes around the bed. He opens a bottle of water and takes a couple of pills from the bottle. I stare at him, completely entranced.

"Where are your clothes?" I ask.

He looks down, seeming to forget that he has none on, and shrugs.

"You'll need to shower soon to get rid of that blood, so I'm prepared to help you." He smirks. Then he crushes the tablets and adds them to the honey on the spoon. He lifts the spoon to my mouth, and I swallow, my eyes on him as I do.

I notice his cock twitch.

I smirk, well, as best I can.

"Can't help it, your mouth turns me on," he says without me saying a word. He pulls the spoon out and hands me the water. "Can you wait at least twenty minutes until the drugs kick in? Might be more tolerable than to get up now." I nod and stay where I am, not wanting to risk lying all the way back down after I have gotten this far. He grabs some pillows and stuffs them behind my back and then heads to the closet.

"I prefer you naked," I say.

He looks at me over his shoulder, his steel-like ass still in view.

What a fabulous, smooth, toned ass he has. I'm jealous.

"Funny, I prefer you naked as well." He returns to the bed and sits down at the end. "Do you want to talk? I suck at it, but if it helps you…" he trails off and simply stares at me.

"Where is he?" I ask, wanting to know where my asshole husband is currently being held.

"In the basement. Still alive. For now."

"Do you plan to kill him?"

He clenches his jaw, then answers with one word, "Yes."

"But those you kill can't be found, right?"

"Correct."

"I'd need him found so I could remarry if I want." My words seem to shock him if his wide eyes are anything to go by.

"You want to marry again?" he asks.

"I don't know. But I want that option. And I don't want him to take anything else from me." He nods solemnly. "Don't worry, Kyson, I won't ask you to marry me." His eyes find mine, and they narrow.

"Would you want to marry me?" he asks seriously.

"I need to pee," I tell him, changing the subject. I know he doesn't want marriage, and I don't even know if I do it again either. But Tony has had so much power over me that it's time I took it back, and this is something I can have.

Kyson stands and moves to my side, then he offers me his hand for support and places his other hand under my arm to assist me up so there is less pressure on my stomach. As I stand, my back curves to try to protect my stomach. All my muscles are aching, and they really don't want to move even one inch. I can tell Kyson is about to tell me to sit back down from the worried look he gets for me.

"I'm fine. I got this," I assure him.

He just looks at me.

I suck in a breath and hope that it will somehow dull the pain.

It doesn't.

Kyson takes it slow with me, each step more careful than the last.

When we finally reach the bathroom, I can see he already has the lid of the toilet lifted. He turns me around, and before I go to sit, he lifts my shirt and tears my underwear off me.

"You didn't have to do that," I say with a smile, but as soon I move to sit, cuss words spill from my mouth. It hurts, but so does my bladder, which is about to burst if I don't relieve myself right now. Ignoring my outburst, he turns to the toilet paper, pulls some off, and hands it to me.

"Thank you."

Kyson nods and stands back while I sit there, peeing for what feels like forever.

"Shower, or can it wait?" he asks.

I raise my eyes and shake my head. "It can wait. I'll try it later."

He assists me back to the bed, and as soon as

I'm lying down again, he fixes the pillows before he grabs the ice pack and walks out of the room.

My phone is sitting on the table beside the bed. I completely forgot about it with everything that happened. I unlock it and note that I have a contact —*Kyson*. He must have added it.

I'm not sure why or what I'm even thinking— maybe it's the drugs—but I download the Facebook app and sign up. Maybe it's because I know that asshole Tony can't hurt me again, and that's a really nice relief to have.

I'm asked to upload a profile picture, but I have no pictures on this phone, and I really don't want to take a photograph of myself right now. I skip that part and add my bio, which is very basic and bland. I put my location as nowhere before I start a search.

After typing in my mother's name, her face pops up immediately. I click on it, not adding her as a friend but checking her public profile. Most things are private, apart from the pictures of me asking me to come home. I gasp, and my hand covers my mouth as tears begin falling down my cheeks. She's begging me to contact them, to come home, and I had no idea.

I keep on scrolling and see that she posts once a week and has for many years. Quickly, I go back and search my father's name and find the exact same thing on his profile, asking me to come home. I didn't think they would ever want to see me again, but maybe that was the poison that Tony put into my head. I did tell him the safe combination and let him break in to steal what he wanted, and I'm to blame for that. It's not something I am proud of.

"Fuck, why are you crying?" Kyson hurries over and places the ice pack on my stomach. He glances at my phone but doesn't take it. "That's your father, right?" he asks.

"Yep," I say, wiping the tears.

"Seems they miss you."

"I miss them too." I click on his profile picture and find a picture of me when I graduated. I look happy. Little did we know this would be one of the last images they'd take of me.

"Message them," he says and clicks the message button.

Unsure, I ask, "What if they think it's a fake or don't read it?"

"I have their info if you want it. Remember, I can track anyone."

I shake my head and start to type a message. It's early, and they will most likely be sleeping and won't respond right away. "What are you typing?" he asks, giving me a bit of privacy by not reading over my shoulder, so I read it out as I type.

"Hi, not sure if this message will come through, but I wanted you to know I am safe. And if you are comfortable with it, I would love to see you again."

I turn to look at Kyson. "Do you think they will see me?" I ask him, my tone filled with hope.

"Of course, they will."

My eyes start to get heavy, and I press send. My heart rate picks up, and I feel nervous.

Really nervous.

But I shouldn't be because my parents love me. Whatever it was that Tony felt for me was anything but love.

"Do you want to be there when I kill him?" Kyson asks.

"No, I do not."

"Do you want to say anything to him before he dies?"

I think on that for a second before I meet his eyes and reply with, "I do."

"Okay. When you're feeling better, we'll make that happen."

"You're just gonna make him wait down there?" I ask, not sure what he has planned.

"Of course. He has nothing better to do." He smiles at me, and I smile back.

I start to fall asleep, and Kyson molds the blankets over me. I want to tell him thank you, but I can't seem to get the words out because sleep takes me.

When I dream, I dream of a white wedding.

My white wedding.

And at the end of the aisle waiting for me...is Kyson.

Something in me tells me that's a lie.

TWENTY-FIVE

Kyson

IT'S three days later when she feels well enough to walk around. Kalilah showered the day after everything went down and hasn't done so since. But when I walk into the bedroom, she is sitting on the end of the bed, trying to get up.

"You want a shower?" I ask.

She looks at me pleadingly, and I walk over to help her. If she were anyone else, she wouldn't be here, and I wouldn't be helping her. In my relationship with Lilly, I never helped her with anything. I was incredibly self-centered, and I expected her to meet *all* of *my* needs. I don't expect anything from Kalilah. Somehow, the roles have reversed, and I'm willing to do anything to make sure she's okay.

My brothers want to know if I really do want

out of this life. I've mentioned it a few times to them, but I haven't really had a straight answer. I enjoy what I do, and that is the biggest issue. How can you enjoy being so fucked-up that the sheer mention of your name makes other people run?

"Do you have plans today?" she asks.

She'd been worried about work, about how she's only just started and has already called in sick. I handled that for her, though. Lady McBeth was more than happy to call on her behalf and say she's working with her for the next few weeks so it doesn't reflect poorly upon her.

And her parents haven't replied.

She checks her phone several times a day, hoping they've messaged her back, but they either haven't seen the message or don't believe it's her. I try not to mention it. I have her parents' cell numbers, and I figure I'll give them another week before I message them myself.

"I have plans to spend it with you, watching that trash you call TV."

She chuckles. "I like it. It's such good trashy TV," she whispers as she steps into the shower.

I remove my clothes and follow behind her. I reach for the soap and grip it in my palm before I turn around and lather up my hands and start to wash her. She turns around to face me and leans in, her head falling to my chest and resting there.

"I really like you, Kyson," she whispers.

"Good, the feeling is mutual," I inform her.

"So, when I say this, I want you to *not* get mad." I look down at her as I wash her back. "I want to move out. I don't want to live here anymore."

"Okay. I'll sell the house, and we can live somewhere else." Problem solved. Easy fix.

"No, I want to live by myself." My hand pauses on her back, and she lifts her head so her eyes meet mine.

"At least for a little while." She smiles. "You can still visit."

I nod and resist the urge to lock her up, to protect her, because that's what I want to do so she can't get hurt again. But if she has proven anything, it's that she is the strongest person I know. Despite everything, she still sees a future for herself.

"You smashed that guy's head in with your boot. You did the same thing that night I was drunk too," she says.

"I did."

"Why?"

"He made me mad," I tell her honestly.

"Do you think you would ever hurt me if I

made you mad?" Her hands are hanging at her sides now, no longer touching me.

"No, never."

"How can you be so sure?"

"Because you make me mad all the time." I grin at her.

"Okay." Her reply is simple, then she smiles and stares at the soap in my hand. "If you're really gentle, you can kiss me." My eyes trace her body, which is still extremely sore.

"It can wait. Gentle isn't in my vocabulary," I say. Her smile drops. Fuck it! "Okay, I'll kiss you." I drop to my knees in the shower. *Fuck, that's painful.*

"What are you doing?"

"You didn't say where to kiss you. And let's be honest, it is my favorite meal." I lean forward and slide my tongue out toward her. She sucks in a breath at the contact and raises her hands to fist them in my hair.

Being careful that she doesn't move too much, I slide my hand down her leg until I tap her ankle. She spreads her legs a little bit wider so I can run my hand back up and slip a finger inside her. I'm mindful of her breathing to ensure she doesn't hurt herself. Kalilah groans and pulls my hair as my tongue circles her clit.

Slipping in a second finger, she spreads her legs even more, and my tongue moves a little faster. I can feel her body start to tense, and I don't want to hurt her, so I slow down, but she tugs at my hair, indicating for me to keep going. So I do what the lady wants, and I fuck her with my mouth. Her pussy tightens around my fingers as they pump in and out of her.

"Kyson..." she says my name as she comes.

When she stops pulsing around my fingers, I pull away, rising from my knees. Once I'm standing in front of her, she opens her eyes, and I brush her wet hair back.

"Feel better, love?"

She grins and leans back into me.

How the fuck did I get by without her?

Kalilah wants to see the asshole the following day.

She is up and walking around more and knows that he's here. I have given him water and nothing more. Even that's a damn luxury the asshole doesn't deserve, but I couldn't let the bastard die on me, not until she has her chance to see and say her piece to him. She follows me down the steps—each one she takes is slower and slower. When I reach the bottom, I flick on the light, and Tony comes into view, tied to the chair and stinking of piss.

"Oh God," she says, covering her mouth.

The asshole's head shoots up at the sound of her voice, and his eyes lock on her. You can see hope bloom in his expression at the sight of this beautiful woman who was once his.

She is careful with each and every step she takes, and I stay by her side as she gets closer to him. His body leans forward as if somehow, he thinks she is there to free him. It's interesting that he would think that, considering everything he's put her through. That he believes he still has a strong enough hold on Kalilah and that she will do anything for him. He saw what his friend did to her, and it didn't even bother him. So for him to even think she is going to save him completely baffles me. Even if she wanted to let him live, I would still kill him. Scum like that asshole doesn't deserve to walk this earth and especially not with her. And there ain't no fucking way she isn't going to be around.

"Kalilah." He says her name, and she stops in her tracks. I lift my hand to her back for support. He notices the movement, and his eyes narrow.

"You cheated on me. Did you forget we're married?" he seethes.

Kalilah flinches back, but I just chuckle.

Tony's eyes find mine.

"You cheated, and you were married. Were you not?" I ask him.

"That's different. Kalilah would only cheat for love. I fucked because she was never in the mood," he grumbles.

"Yet you still forced me anyway," she says quietly.

"You liked it." He smiles evilly.

"You are the worst fuck I've ever had," she shoots back, chin raised in defiance.

There's my girl, and I'm so proud of her.

"I want you to die knowing I am good, that I've made a new, better life for myself. Despite you trying to control me, claim me as if I were your prize, and isolate me from everyone. It didn't work in the long run. I contacted my parents, I have made friends, and I have *great sex*." She smirks at that, and I do too, knowing she's talking about me.

"You fuck him? *Him?*" he screams.

"It's best you go and meet up with Alaska, love. I have things I need to take care of." I lean in and kiss her lips, griping her cheeks as I do, so he can

229

see that she is mine. I pull away and touch them one last time, smiling at her. "I will see you tonight."

She nods, and I watch as she heads to the stairs.

"How could you leave me here with him after everything I've done for you?" he screams. "You slut." She tenses at his words but keeps on going.

I walk over and punch his face at the use of that word. She doesn't look back, and when she's gone, I step in front of him and lean down.

"It's time to play." I smirk.

The asshole starts shaking his head, but that won't get him anywhere.

"You must think of yourself as a big man because no one ever says no to you." I stand to my full height. "I have one brother who loves the use of knives." I walk to the table. "And the other loves guns *and* knives, but for different reasons." I lift up both items in my hands and move to take the seat opposite him. He eyes the items as I sit. "Me, I am pretty much always a fight-with-my-fists-and-boots type of man, you know? I am quick with my hands. And the boots to the face... Well, it simply helps with my anger issues. Supposedly we all have anger issues. Who knew?" I shrug, staring at him.

"Let me go. I will pay you and never contact her again," he begs.

"Yeah, that's not going to happen. You see, you are a liar. We all know this. And I am not a man to be fooled." I lift the knife and flip it between my fingers. He watches every move before I grip the handle and fling it so hard that it embeds itself deep in his shoulder. "Shit, I need better aim." I get up as his eyes go wide with shock, then I pull the knife out, and he screams. I calmly sit back down. "I'm sure I can do better than that. My brother would not be proud of me." I smile and flip the knife again between my fingers before I walk over to him and place my lips to his forehead before I move back, raise my eyes to him, and throw it again. This time I hit him directly between the legs. My intended target.

He howls like the bitch he is.

And soon enough, I lift the gun and smirk as I shoot right between the eyes.

Fucking dickhead, calling my woman a slut.

TWENTY-SIX

Kalilah
_____

IT'S THREE WEEKS LATER, and I'm back at work and moving into my own place. It's nice, though Kyson doesn't seem too pleased to have me leave his home. But he still bought me furniture, which I find funny, and he also tried to give me his car. I told him no, but that I will borrow it until I can get my own. He simply rolled his eyes at me as we carried my new couch inside.

My parents finally responded. I look down at the message again.

Is it really you?

I haven't replied.

It's been two days since I received their message, and I keep typing something up and then deleting it.

"A simple 'yes' should suffice," Kyson says, sitting on the couch. He told me Tony wasn't going to be an issue again. The police contacted me, saying they had found his body and that they were sorry for my loss. I'm officially a widow, and that feels damn good to say. I'm no longer married to the devil.

"But what if they don't believe me?" I ask.

Alaska walks in and flips her hair. "It's green," I say, shocked.

"Yep, my mood changed," she replies.

"To what?" I ask her, confused.

"Green with envy," she says proudly.

"Of?" I question, still not understanding.

"That you get a choice if Kyson moves in or not. Zuko forced himself into my place."

"Let's not forget you set my house on fire," Zuko adds, shaking his head as he hands me a bag. "It's from her." He nods to Alaska.

"You were supposed to say from us, you fool." She rolls her eyes at him.

"Yeah, what she said." He sits on the couch next to his brother.

"Did you really burn his house down?" I ask.

"Yep. Lit that match and sat on his grass and

watched that fucker burn. Taught him not to mess with me again."

"You are my hero." I smile at her.

"I want it noted that I like my house," Kyson interjects.

"Well, don't piss Kalilah off, and you should be fine." Alaska smiles and then points to the bag. "I brought you a bunch of sex toys. You know, since you will be alone now."

"You what?" Kyson says.

"Oh fuck!" Zuko shakes his head, realizing he gave me the bag.

"Yep. Best gift ever." She claps her hands. "Zuko likes it rough, so I tried to not go overboard with you."

"So does Kyson," I say with an eye roll.

"I've been gentle since you've been hurt," he says proudly.

"You tried to tear my hair from my head last night," I remind him.

"Yes, but I didn't spank you." He winks.

"We're leaving," Zuko announces as he stands.

"Sit back down," Alaska states with an eye roll.

He obeys, and I smile.

"I have to go and see the doctor. I gave him my

blood the other day, and I keep forgetting. Could you drive me?" I say to Alaska.

"I'll take you," Kyson offers.

"No, it's fine."

"She asked me, not you." Alaska grins at him like she has won some super fantastic lottery prize.

"Fuck, you annoy me," Kyson rumbles, and Zuko punches him for talking to Alaska that way.

I'm not sure why I don't want Kyson to come, but I need to try doing things without him again.

"Okay, let's go. The boys can finish putting that dining set together."

Kyson gets up, cups the back of my head, and kisses my lips. "I want to go," he whines.

"No." I push him away playfully, then grab my things and follow Alaska to her car.

"Any reason you don't want him to come?" she asks.

"He needs to breathe on his own for a bit."

"Yeah, that doesn't really happen with these men." She chuckles. "They breathe for you."

And I believe her knowing it is all or nothing with them.

They have always been that way with each other, so why would it be any different when they like someone? But then I remember Lilly and wonder why he's different with me.

"And it's okay to tell them to stop, just so you are aware." Alaska looks at me as she slows down.

"It's not that I want him to stop. I like having him there… It's comforting. It's just… I feel free for the first time in a long time, and I don't want to rely on a man to feel that way."

She nods in understanding. "Okay, yeah, I like the sound of that." As we pull up to the doctor's house, she asks, "Want me to come in?"

"Thanks, but I won't be long," I tell her.

I head inside, and the doctor greets me right away. "Hello, Kalilah. This should be a quick visit." He shuts the door behind me. "Everything looks great, but there is one thing."

"Yeah?" I ask hesitantly.

"You're pregnant."

I shake my head.

I can't be.

"Nope, we use protection."

We always use protection.

Except when…

Oh fuck! It must register on my face.

"It only takes one time," is all he says. "I do have options for you."

"That's okay. Thanks anyway. I should go." Doc nods and opens the door.

Alaska smiles as I get in the car. "That was fast. Everything good?"

I look down at my phone as Alaska starts the car, and I bring up my messages. Both of my parents have messaged me now. I haven't replied to either of them.

I look at my mother's last message and write, *I'm pregnant.*

It's probably not the smartest way to say, *yes, it's me,* but I had to tell someone, and my mother is the first person I wanted to tell.

My phone dings in my hand, and it's her.

Can I call?

I turn to Alaska, who's now driving and still waiting for me to answer her.

"Sorry, it's my mother. I haven't spoken to her in a very long time."

"Don't apologize. Go ahead, of course."

I message back, *I'm in the car. I'll call you soon.*

She sends me a love emoji.

"Do you think you can drop me off at the café? I want to do some work and reply to a few emails."

"You want me to stay and talk shit?" she jokes.

"No, but thank you."

She doesn't argue with me or ask any more questions.

When she drops me off, I wave goodbye and go in and sit down at the back. Inhaling a deep breath, I call my mom.

If I think about it too long, I'm not sure I will do it. My hands are shaky, and my breathing is uneven.

"Kalilah." My mother's voice echoes through the phone. "Is it really you?"

"Yes," I manage to murmur out.

"Oh, thank God! And you are well?"

I think about her question. *Am I well?* I'm not really sure how to answer that. I haven't been well. I have been anything but well. But I don't know if I want to share all that with her just yet.

"And Tony? He's okay with you calling us?"

I hate that name.

I hate everything that name stands for.

I hate that this is what it's come down to.

"I'm not with Tony anymore, Mom."

"Oh, sorry. We just assumed…"

"It's okay, but Tony is dead."

She gasps. "Oh, he, we are so sorry."

"It's fine. He was an asshole." I tell her the

truth. She's quiet, so I continue with, "I'm sorry I did all those awful things."

"It wasn't you," she says.

"I know, but I allowed him to do it."

"You didn't know any better. He was, as you say, an asshole." And I just know she is smiling by the sound of her voice. "But you said you were pregnant?" she asks. "Is it not his?"

"No, it's not. I left Tony over a year ago," I admit. "It's the man who saved me from him."

"Oh. Well, I like him already. Are you both excited?" she asks.

Excited. What a funny word to describe someone's feelings.

Am I excited? I don't really know.

I glance down at my flat stomach and can't imagine something growing in there. But there is.

"When I found out I was pregnant with you, I was flustered. I didn't know what to do," she says, filling the silence. "I never thought we would have kids. We tried for years and then kind of gave up. Then one day, I realized I was late. And by then, you were almost the size of an apple. How I missed all those months is beyond me. But, damn, seeing you on the ultrasound was amazing. That's when it became real for me."

I sit there wiping my eyes, listening to her beautiful voice.

"I'm sorry it took me so long to contact you. I thought you wouldn't want to hear from me after… well, everything."

"You'll soon realize a mother's love knows no bounds," she shares. Then she asks, "Are you still with him, that man?"

"Yes."

"Okay. Well, when you're comfortable with it, your father and I would love to see you."

"Next week?" I suggest. "I have work this week, but I have a few days off next week."

"Oh, yes."

"Can I come to you?"

"Of course. Your partner is welcome as well."

"I'll talk to you soon. Goodbye, Mom."

I hang up, and my phone immediately rings. I see Kyson's name flash on the screen. I choose not to answer it as I sit there staring at my phone as though it might just poison me. Then I start googling about pregnancy, and that's where I stay for the next hour before I hear his voice.

"You get lost?" Kyson leans over and places a kiss on my forehead.

"How did you find me?"

"Alaska told me. Wasn't sure if you were still here but figured I'd try my luck since it's getting late. How did it go with the doctor?" he asks, sitting next to me.

I hide my screen and look up at him. "I spoke to my mother," I tell him. "I'm going to visit them next week." He smiles at that. "Alone." His smile drops.

"You don't want me to come?" he asks, sounding hurt.

"No, I don't."

He pulls away from me. "Are you ready? I gotta drop you off and go to work."

I can feel his mood change. He licks his lips as he stands, not offering me his hand. I can tell he's annoyed, and usually, that would bother me. But I don't have the energy to argue with him right now.

"I can find my own way back," I tell him.

He hesitates for a moment, then looks me in the eyes before he shakes his head. "Message me to let me know you got there safe," he says before he turns and walks out. I watch him from the window as he gets in his car. He bangs the steering wheel a few times and then drives off.

I feel bad, but then I remember....

This life is now my journey, and no other man will control it.

TWENTY-SEVEN

Kyson

"FUCK, man, he's dead. Enough! We need to go."
Kenzo pulls at me, but I don't budge. "Anger
issues," he says as I push him off me.

"Fuck you!"

"So what, she wanted to be alone. Do you
blame her?" He shakes his head. "Before her, all
you wanted to do was be alone as well. We Hunters
love solitude." He pauses and looks back at Zuko.
"Except him. He is obsessed."

She left last week, and I haven't seen or heard
from her since that day in the café.

No text messages.

No calls.

"Have you messaged her at least?" Kenzo asks.

"Of course I have."

"Pops is asking why you aren't taking his calls," Zuko asks me, breaking his silence. Then he turns to Kenzo. "You are to clean this up. You've been doing more jobs for Pops than anyone, and don't even deny it."

"You have?" I ask Kenzo, surprised. We all do some solo jobs, but I didn't realize he was doing that many of them.

"Not since you told me." He means about the photographs and other evidence. "I did some digging of my own, and let's say I am *not* liking what I've been finding." He cracks his neck.

"He took advantage of our loyalty," Zuko says and then steps up to Kenzo. "Sort it," he tells him before he strides off.

The cleaners arrive and nod to us as we pass them and get into the car. Kenzo's phone starts buzzing a little way down the road. He shows me the screen. I shrug, and he places it on speaker.

"Kenzo..." I grind my teeth. "I think you and I need to have a talk. Have you been looking into me?" Kenzo's eyes lift to mine. Not my problem—it's all fucking his. I did my job and found out stuff they had no idea about. They told me to leave it, so now it's their fucking problem. "You know I get notified when someone searches my name, and I traced it back to you."

"Impossible, nothing can be traced to me," Kenzo says and then hangs up. "He's bluffing. Even his best men wouldn't be able to trace me, and I know that for a fact." I believe him. He's basically a genius when it comes to anything computers. Not really sure where that came from, but I'm glad he has the skills we lack in that department. "Drop me at the club."

"Fucking hell," Zuko mutters, turning the car around.

When we arrive at the club, I get out with Kenzo. He looks surprised at first but says nothing when we walk in. Zuko leaves to get back to Alaska.

The doors open to reveal Avani standing there.

Grayson, the owner, is one of the only men we can stand, or trust for that matter. He used to do jobs for us that we didn't have the time for. They call him the bogeyman, but lately, he's been wifed up with Avani.

"Boys, what a pleasure. Since you're here, would you assist Grayson? He's having issues with a bachelor party that doesn't know when to quit."

I follow Kenzo inside. He frequents the club a lot, so he knows where to go. Straight out the back, past the colored rooms. Kenzo loves the red room, but it's the blue room—the water room—where we find Grayson standing on the stairs that lead to the jacuzzi. He turns around when he spots us, not saying a word before he looks back to the men.

"Get the fuck up and get out. Last warning," he tells the men.

Three men sit in the jacuzzi, all with glasses of champagne in their hands, which is not allowed, and a woman on each of their laps. And you can tell the women don't want to be there, but they're being held in place by the three dumbasses.

Most people know better than to come into this club and fuck with Grayson. For a start, Grayson once killed a guy for having champagne in the blue room. He has a reputation for taking no shit in here. It's also what makes the club so popular. But these men clearly have had too much to drink and couldn't give two shits regarding who is standing above them, telling them to get the fuck out.

One even starts to laugh, and I watch as his hand moves up and grips the woman's tit a little too hard.

A scream comes from her—*she clearly never signed up for this*—and I can see the terror in her face.

Before anyone even notices, Kenzo starts

moving, and no one can stop him as he takes his small pocketknife and stabs the man in the shoulder.

"Get out. *Now*," Grayson growls again at the men as Kenzo pulls the knife out and steps back like he did nothing at all. The other men get angry and push the women off them. They stand completely naked, ready to fight, and all Grayson does is calmly roll up his sleeves. "If you go down this path, remember *you* chose it."

The women jump out of the tub and run out of the room, leaving just us men. I smirk, knowing I don't have to do anything. Grayson could kill them all by himself. But it's Kenzo who is thirsty, his head dropping to the side as he watches them.

"We'll leave," the one cradling his injured shoulder says as he looks at Kenzo, terror in his eyes. "We'll leave. We only wanted to have some fun."

"Now would be a good time to go," Grayson says, stepping out of the way so they can walk down the stairs. They hurry past us, grab their clothes, and are out the door.

"I'll follow to make sure they leave," Kenzo says, trailing behind them.

Grayson turns to face me. "Met your new

woman the other day. Avanti said she's nice." He leans down and presses a button, draining the tub. "Is she another Lilly?"

"Absolutely fucking not."

"So, she's an Avanti." He smirks. "Makes you crazy and insane, but you couldn't imagine your life without her." He chuckles. "Be prepared for the non-stop headaches and the trouble that follows them around. They know how to grab their men by the balls and take control."

"She left," I tell him.

"So? You're Kyson Hunter. When haven't you gone after what you want? Why are you still standing here talking to me? I ain't gonna suck your dick." He chuckles at his own words before he saunters out of the room, leaving me standing in the blue room alone.

I pull my phone out of my pocket and press call.

She doesn't answer.

She hasn't been replying to my text messages either.

Did she forget that I can find her, no matter where she is, no matter if she is in hiding?

Jumping onto the airline website, I book the next flight out.

I guess it's time to meet the parents.

What the fuck is she doing to me?

Grayson is partially right, apart from the fact that she might be crazy or trouble. I think she's more sane than anyone gives her credit for and more put together than anyone of her age, but that doesn't surprise me with everything she's been through.

She is strong, that one, and it makes me want to...

Oh, fuck—love her even more.

TWENTY-EIGHT

Kalilah

I'M NOT sure that I ever really want to leave here again, but I know that I must. I'm an adult now, and I have a job that I like and an apartment that I haven't fully settled into quite yet. And a man who I have news to tell.

When I first saw my parents again, we cried, and it felt like the tears would never end. They wanted to know everything, but I could only give them so much. Some things are better left unsaid. But the pieces of me I was willing to share with them, I did. About Kyson, and how he saved me, in ways that would put a parent at ease; how he was willing to help me when I was at my rock bottom. I skipped over a lot of the bad with Tony, but I think that's for the best. Of course, they asked me about him, and I told them I was glad he was no longer in my life, and when I did my mother touched my hand and squeezed it.

She knew, she always knew, he was never right for me.

But young love is hard.

Especially when that person knows how to control you.

My father, well that was a different story. He had to walk out of the room when we spoke of Tony, and I could tell the topic of my husband upset him greatly. And I don't blame him. When he would come back into the room he would walk over and kiss me on the top of the head and tell me how much he loved me.

It's nice to know that no matter what, they love me.

We went to my first ultrasound to see how far along I was. The sonographer asked me why the father wasn't there, and I wasn't quite sure how to tell her that I hadn't told him yet.

If I am being perfectly honest with myself, I am afraid of Kyson's reaction.

At least, that's what I keep telling myself.

I'm not sure if I'm more scared to admit the fact that I am pregnant out loud to him or what his reaction will be. His world is dark, and not really fit to raise a child within.

I don't know how to tell him that either.

I don't know how to share my thoughts with him.

I don't think of him in any way like Tony because they're two completely different people. I was scared of Tony. But with Kyson, I'm more afraid of hurting him, which is laughable considering who he is. He has showed me kindness, and the only other man in this world to ever do that is my father.

"Um...dear? There is a man at the door asking for you." I get off the couch and head to the door, thinking it's a delivery of some sort. But the only thing I've ordered while I've been here is food. "He is *very* handsome." My feet freeze in place before I reach the door, and I slowly turn my head toward her.

"Does he look menacing?" I ask, and she scrunches her nose up with a slight smirk.

"I don't think so. He was very polite." She smiles. *Okay then, that can't be Kyson.*

I get to the door and see Kyson standing there looking at me from the other side.

"Hello, love."

"*Ohh*," my mother breathes out as she reaches for the screen door and pulls it open. "You must be the father. It's so nice to finally meet you. We had the first ultrasound the other day, and they said the baby looks healthy." Kyson's eyes find mine, then fall to my stomach, but he can't see anything because it's still quite early in the pregnancy. It takes him a moment to recover.

"I've heard so much about you. Would you mind if I stole your daughter for ten minutes? I have some information I need to share with her," he says directly to my mom.

"Of course," my mother gushes.

Kyson offers me his hand, and I look at it, unsure if I should take it, before I place my hand in his and step outside.

"We'll be back," I tell my mother as we walk out.

I'm barefoot as he leads me to his car. He opens the door and waves for me to slide in. I do so, and he closes me inside. Kyson walks around the hood to his side, gets in, and starts the car, turning the music up but not too loud. He grips the steering wheel hard and blows out a breath.

"Kyson—"

"How long have you known?" he interrupts, not looking my way.

"I found out the day you came to the café to find me."

His knuckles start to turn white on the steering wheel from the force of his grip.

"Did you intend to tell me, or were you planning something else?"

"I wasn't planning anything. I was trying to get my head together."

He turns and faces me, his eyes dark, but I don't feel afraid.

"I want to know these things," he insists.

"Do you even want kids?" I ask.

"That's not the damn point. I am not *him*. You tell me things. That's what we do." He breathes deeply and then tries to reassure me by repeating, "You tell me things, Kalilah. Do you get it?"

"I do. And you need to know I'm keeping the baby, but I don't expect anything from you," I manage to squeak out.

He looks away, and I can't read his face. *Is he mad because of what I said?* I know I'm young, and what we have is new, so I really don't expect anything from him. I lift my hand to put it on his shoulder but pull it back. I'm not sure what is the right thing to do in this situation.

"You're keeping it?" he asks.

"Yes."

"You know who I am. Who my family is and what we do," he says.

"Yes, you know I do."

He stares out at the house—the house I grew up in—and sees the white shutters on the windows, the brown brick, and the wraparound porch. It's an average-looking home. There's nothing too fancy about it, but it's somewhere I feel extremely comfortable. I can see him staring again, going quiet, probably thinking of what to say next.

Him and me both.

I was planning to tell him when I got home and worked out my plan of attack. You can't just jump up and say to someone you slept with a few times, "Oh, and by the way, I'm pregnant with your baby, and I'm keeping it." I suppose some people can, but my situation is somewhat different. The man I'm seeing is an assassin, a trained killer, not that I think for a second he would kill me, but the situation is definitely different.

"I didn't have this kind of life," he says, nodding to the house.

My parents in the living room, watching television, waiting for me to come back inside. They'll want to know more about Kyson to see if he's different from Tony.

He is…

In so many ways.

"Is this the life you want?" Kyson asks, and I see the worry in his eyes as the words leave his mouth. I get it. He's worried that he won't be able to give me *this* life.

"I like where my life is heading. I like my new place, your car that I get to drive, and I like having sex with you." I smile at him. "Can we not just like the now?"

His eyes drop to my stomach. "It's not the now I'm worried about." Kyson gets out of the car and walks around to my side. I sit there, confused, before he reaches my door and opens it. "Introduce me to your parents."

"What about your parents?" I ask.

"Dead. I couldn't care less. It's yours I'm concerned about." I take his offered hand and step out with his help.

"I'll give you three months to live by yourself before you are *mine*," he states.

"My lease is for six months," I reply.

"We will shorten it." He shuts the door, not letting go of my hand as we walk to the house. I almost trip on the driveway, and he catches me. I look up at him and start laughing, and his eyes narrow like I'm a crazy person, and I lift my hand over my mouth.

"How times have changed. That one time you let me fall on my face."

"You annoyed me," he says like it was obvious.

"Yeah, and you'd just killed someone," I whisper.

"Kalilah." We both turn at the sound of my mother's voice at the door—thankfully out of earshot—with my father standing behind her with his arms crossed over his chest, trying to be intimidating.

I wonder if Kyson is ever intimidated. I doubt it.

I approach with Kyson's hand still in mine, and he gives it a little squeeze as we near them.

"This is Kyson," I say and smile.

"Son." My father nods his head and offers his hand.

Kyson takes and shakes it.

"It's good to meet you. Kalilah has spoken of you both fondly," Kyson says, and my heart warms at his words.

"She's barely mentioned you. What do you do for work?" I tense at my father's terse words, but Kyson simply squeezes my hand.

"I'm a contractor. I run my own business."

My father nods in approval. "And your family? Your parents?"

"Parents have passed away. My brothers all live close by back home," Kyson says.

My father looks at me. "And you like his brothers?"

I remember the night with Kenzo on the couch. "Yes, both are lovely." *In their own way*, I add to myself. Kenzo in how close he is to his brothers, and Zuko with how close he is to his brothers and how much he adores Alaska.

"Let's go inside. It's getting dark," my father says.

"It's so nice to meet you. Sorry about him. Now he has his girl back he is worried he won't see her again," my mother gushes, reaching out and laying her hand on Kyson's shoulder. "You wouldn't stop her from seeing us, would you?"

My mother and I look a lot alike. Same color hair and the same build, but I have my father's eyes.

"Never," Kyson says, and I believe him. "Family is important. It's why I work with my brothers and would trust them with my life." He isn't joking. They literally do, then they kill the ones they don't like. *Funny, but whatever.*

My mother's hand goes to her heart.

"I love that. Her ex…" She shakes her head.

"Yes, Tony. I met him."

My father stops, turns around, and asks, "You did?"

"Yes, and he was worse than awful. So I showed him exactly how to treat a lady."

My father smirks. "What did you do?" I'm sure my father would be happy to know Tony is dead, but I know Kyson won't share that part with him.

"I hit him, hard, after he spoke to her like his possession."

My father nods, smiling, then turns to me. "I'm glad you aren't with him anymore, dear."

"Me too," I answer.

"Want a beer, son?" my father offers.

He likes Kyson.

I know he does.

"Yes, sir."

"Oh, please don't call me that, it makes me feel old. Call me Hampton," my father says, giving him his first name.

Kyson releases my hand and follows my father to the bar fridge and I hear my father ask him more questions as I turn to face my mother.

"Your father likes this one. He never liked Tony."

"I like him too," I tell her, smiling.

"Yeah, he seems a bit rough around the edges. But I can see by the way he looks at you he thinks the ground you walk on is magical." She gets a dreamy look in her eyes as she says, "Your father still thinks that about me and I love it." Mom pulls me into the kitchen and starts cutting the cake she was baking before Kyson showed up. "Do you think he may stay for a little while?"

"Yes, I think he will."

"He won't be needed at work?"

I shake my head and tell her, "But I have to go back to work soon."

She reaches over the counter and clasps my hand. "I'm so proud of you. Look how far you have come." And her words make me feel good. Really good. It's crazy how a few simple words from someone you love can make all the difference. I'm still trying to understand and process it. Tony never complimented me. All he ever did was talk down to me. And after so long without praise, I guess you forget what normal is and only expect the worst.

Well, not anymore.

I deserve the best.

TWENTY-NINE

Kyson

KALILAH'S PARENTS ARE NICE, and they clearly love and miss her tremendously. I'm not really sure what that feels like, but I'm glad it makes her happy.

I ended up spending the night, and her mother asked that I sleep in the spare room. Kalilah tried to say it would be fine if we shared, but I didn't want to disrespect them, so I slept in the spare room across from her and didn't move all night. Though when I finally woke, she was lying next to me, her leg swung over mine, and her hair fanned out over my chest.

She's supposed to go home with me today.

I've been thinking of how I'm going to tell my brothers about the baby and what I'm going to do. The idea of leaving *the life* is even more at the forefront of my brain as well as the notion that I had to choose one life or the other might have been a decision I was planning to make for all the wrong reasons. Kalilah hasn't asked me to make a choice, and she knows all about me and what I do to earn my money. It doesn't really seem to bother her all that much.

"Kalilah." I nudge her, and she jumps up, covering her mouth. She goes to turn, but before she can move, she throws up all over the bed...and me.

"Fuck."

"Sorry," she chokes out, running for the bathroom.

I get up to follow her, careful not to touch my vomit-covered chest while trying not to retch myself.

Jesus! That shit stinks.

Bad.

"Everything okay?" Her father pops his head in, already dressed, and looks around the room. I hear Kalilah spewing again and push past her father and into the bathroom, where she is hunched over the toilet. I grab her hair, which is already covered in vomit, and hold it back.

"I'm sorry, I didn't know," she whimpers.

"It's fine," I tell her, brushing her hair back out of her face.

"I'll get you some clean water." I hear her father from the doorway and catch a glimpse of him just before he walks off.

"Can you move?" I ask.

"I—" She goes to stand but heaves again, throwing up whatever remains in her stomach. When she stops, her father steps in and sets the water on the counter.

"Your mother left to get some fresh bread. What can I do?" he asks, sympathy showing on his features.

"I'm going to shower her. Maybe you could bring some fresh towels?" I ask, and his face lights up, happy to help. After grabbing some towels and bringing them back, her father steps out and closes the door behind him.

Still gripping her hair, I step away and start the shower, making sure it's warm before I help her stand.

She turns to me and meets my eyes. "I'm so sorry." Tears spill down her cheeks.

"It's done. It's just payback for the river I made you swim in, right?"

She smiles at me as I reach for her shirt and pull

it over her head. I didn't sleep with a shirt on, only trousers, which I manage to get off before I help her with her underwear. We step into the shower, and I start to wash her.

"I was hoping I'd skipped over the morning sickness. Mom said she had it bad with me and even had to be hospitalized at one stage because she couldn't keep anything down." I smooth her wet hair back under the water as she talks. "Let's hope I don't get the same thing. Can you imagine me at work spewing on a customer?" She shivers at the thought. "I couldn't sleep last night, so I crept into bed with you."

"I know." I grin at her. "I could tell from last night's dinner that ended up on my chest." Her lips tug up into a smile, and I know all is right in the world. She pushes up against me and kisses my chest.

"My mother also told me that some women get really aroused while pregnant." She grabs my hand and pulls it down between her legs. "Can you tell?" She starts rubbing against my hand before I find her entrance and slip a finger inside. She moans.

"Fuck, you're wet."

Kalilah drops her head back under the water and rinses her mouth out, all the while gripping me to her and riding my hand. I reach for the removable showerhead and take it off, turning it to a more powerful setting, then I point it down at her clit. Her eyes open wide, and I slip a second finger in.

"That's making me feel so much better," she whispers, knowing full well her parents could be out there.

"Good, that's what we want." She nods eagerly as she moves her hips, and I finger fuck her hard. Watching her come is truly something magical.

I fucking love it.

"I love you," I tell her.

She freezes for a moment, then pushes the showerhead away and basically climbs me. I lift her, and she quickly finds my cock and slides straight onto it. She bites my shoulder and rides me up and down. I grip her thighs, helping her, and slip a finger into her ass to make her move even faster.

Just as she starts to come, she bites down hard enough to break the skin on my shoulder, but I don't stop. Her pussy is milking my cock like nobody's business, and the water is spraying everywhere, probably soaking the bathroom.

But I don't care.

Fuck it all.

As she comes down from the pleasure high, her

body goes slack, and I have to take over. I fuck her like the good girl she is.

And then when I'm done...

"I want to marry you," I declare.

She throws her head back and laughs.

Little does she know I am *not* joking.

THIRTY

Kalilah
_____

MY PARENTS LIKE HIM A LOT.

I'm not all that surprised.

I like him a lot too.

Kyson jokes about marrying me, and I don't want to tell him that those words alone give me heart palpitations. And not in a good way. Not that I'm afraid to marry him, specifically. I'm more afraid of marriage itself, considering how my last marriage turned out. Kyson hasn't expressed his worries to me, but I can tell they're there—it's extremely evident.

"Yours or mine?" he asks, driving back from the airport.

I haven't been sick again since that morning. And I'm so thankful. I suck at holding vomit down.

Never mastered it. It's more like, *surprise bitches, better run*.

"Mine," I tell him, then add, "You've been quiet."

"Can I invite my brothers over?" he asks, looking my way briefly before turning back to the road.

"Yes, you know you can."

He pulls up to my place, helps me out of the car, and carries my bag up the stairs. I let him while I unlock the door before we walk in. "Oh, I forgot to share with you, but it's not much…" I reach into my bag and pull out the sonogram. "I want to find out if it's a boy or girl, but it's too early right now," I tell him, handing him the picture.

He studies for a minute, then says, "I have no idea what I'm looking at."

"That's our baby, growing inside of me," I say, pointing at the heart. "Why are your brothers coming over? Everything okay?"

"I'm telling them I'm quitting," he says matter-of-factly, and my head whips up so I can meet his eyes.

"Why?"

"I don't need the money, and it's what's best for you."

"Don't bring me into this. I have no issue with what you do. Just don't tell me any gory details, and we will be fine," I insist. "So don't you quit because of me! That's not fair."

"I've been thinking about quitting for a while… way before we met. This just pushed me farther in that direction."

"I'm not her, Kyson. This…" I wave a hand between us. "We aren't like what you and she were."

He steps closer to me and grabs my shoulder. "You and I are nothing like that, and I know it. I respect you. And I want to do what's best for not only you but the baby. And us."

"Okay, so don't quit. I know how much you love what you do."

"What about when your parents dig further and ask me more about my job?" he asks, letting me go.

"You can give them some form of the truth. I don't expect you to lie. You are a contractor, of sorts, and you search for people who can't be found," I tell him, smiling. "See, that was easy."

"And what about the nights when I come home worked up and covered in blood?" he argues.

"You will learn to respect that you shouldn't bring blood in the house and to use a hose." I turn and walk to the kitchen, needing some water. My stomach is upset.

"Are you okay?" He's behind me before I can even open the fridge.

"Yes, just need water."

He reaches in before I can and grab the jug, then pours me a glass.

"I can do that."

"You're pale," he points out as I take the water from him and drink it, the coolness helping my throat a little.

A knock comes at the door, and Kyson goes to open it, checking over his shoulder to ensure I'm okay. I hear his brothers before I see them as they both come in and head straight for the sofa.

I stay in the kitchen when they talk. Kyson keeps looking my way, but I feel better already. It's just the start of the pregnancy, and it will get better with time.

I hope.

"What's so urgent?" Zuko asks.

"I was going to quit," he starts, then focuses his gaze on me. "But she said no."

At that, I have the attention of all of them.

"You love it. You all do." I wave a hand. "Don't

even look at me like I'm the bad guy." I put the water to my lips and drink some more.

"I'll stay, for now," Kyson says.

I give him my best eye roll and see Kenzo smirk at me.

"What's wrong with you?" he asks, eyeing me.

"I'm pregnant," I say matter-of-factly.

"Yeah, sounds about right," he says teasingly and turns to Kyson, who is staring at me like I dropped a bomb.

"Shit, you really are?" Kenzo looks at me, surprised.

"I did say I was. Did you think I was lying?"

"Well, yes." He shrugs, and Zuko is watching Kyson.

"Is this what you want?" Kenzo asks Kyson.

We're all quiet for a beat because, to the twins, Zuko is their everything. They followed his path and have been with him since the beginning.

"If it's what she wants," Kyson says.

"Nope. I told him he didn't have to stay," I state.

Kyson stares at me.

"Didn't have to stay, " he says, shaking his head. "I stay for you and whatever it is you want." His eyes go a little softer. "If you want the baby, we will have the baby."

"You shouldn't have a baby just because I am."

He lets out a heavy sigh. "You know that makes no sense."

"I know, but it did in my head. What I am saying is…just because I'm having *your baby* it doesn't mean you have to be a part of *our life.*"

"But I want you in my life," he argues. "And that baby is a part of you…and me."

"Yes, it will be." I nod.

"So, I'll probably love it more than you because it won't talk smack to me." He smiles like he's won. He hasn't.

I win.

It's my favorite thing about us—he lets me win.

The guys stand and walk over to me.

"We hate kids. And I hated these two as kids even more," Zuko says, motioning to his brothers. "It could be twins, you know."

Oh fuck! I didn't even think of that.

Zuko smiles when he sees the sheer terror on my face. "I'll like this kid, but don't have any more." He nods and walks out.

Kenzo grins widely at me before following Zuko.

"Breathe," Kyson reminds me.

"Twins," I say through a staggered breath.

Fuck. How did that not occur to me?

"I don't want my vagina to be stretched that much by two kids."

"Our mother had a C-section. We came early," he informs me. "She was on crack too, so that could have been part of the reason." He shrugs, making my eyes bulge at his words. "What? I never said she was a good mother... Look how we all turned out."

"Yeah, fucked-up."

"Hey, at least we don't beat and control our women."

"No, you just push them in rivers."

"Oh, for fuck's sake, I will never live that down."

I give him an eye roll.

"Only when they talk back." He licks his lips. "Now, should we try for another baby?" Kyson steps real close and presses himself against me and I lay my hand on his chest.

"You know you can't impregnate me again when I'm already pregnant," I tell him, leaning in close to his lips. "I want dirty public sex," I whisper. He pulls back and grabs my hand, tugging me toward the door, and I giggle as I follow him. When we get to the street, he slips off his jacket and wraps it around me before he pulls me close.

"It's late. Where are we going?" I ask.

"The theme park is still open. That's where we're going."

"I'm pregnant. No rides," I remind him.

"You can ride this ride, trust me." And I have a feeling he's talking about him.

It doesn't take long until we get out of the car at the theme park. He strides up to the ticket counter, and the attendant lets him know the park closes in an hour. Kyson nods and pulls me through the gate. The place is crowded. Families and couples are everywhere as they wait for the fireworks. He tugs me along until we get to where the fireworks display is to start, where he finds a spot along the fence between a few families. He leans against the fence and pulls me into him.

His hands slide under my coat as he rests his head on my shoulder. "How dirty we talking?" he whispers.

Maybe I let the words slip out a little too fast earlier. *He can't be serious about this.*

His hand under my coat finds my skirt and slips beneath it. I gasp as he touches my clit—I'm super sensitive there.

"Shhh, love, the man next to us turned this way for a moment." I open my eyes like I'm not being touched intimately in public, and he isn't about to make me come as his fingers slide up and down my pussy, then tease my opening.

He slips a finger inside, and I try to compose myself, I really do, but he shushes me again, so I must have spoken or made a noise without realizing. The fireworks start, and before I know it, everything is loud, everyone is looking up, and I turn around to face him. I place my arms around his neck, and he lifts me, the jacket covering my ass from hanging out, and I pretend to look at the fireworks to the side as I whisper in his ear, "Fuck me, Kyson."

"You don't have to ask me twice." He holds me without any effort with one hand and slides his other between us. My underwear is already to the side, so when I feel his cock at my entrance, I take him in.

Everyone is standing and clapping as the last of the fireworks finish. I clap too, behind his head, pretending I'm also happy about the fireworks, when in reality, I'm wondering if anyone knows that his cock is currently deep inside of me. I bounce and scream, "Wahoo!" throwing my head back at the fireworks as he chuckles in my ear.

"Security is coming," he whispers.

"Oh my God, get out of me," I whisper-shriek.

He pulls out, lowers me gently to my feet, then tucks himself back in. He makes sure my skirt is in place before he turns and leads me in the opposite direction from, I'm guessing, where the security was approaching. Kyson starts to walk faster, and I have to jog to keep up. He veers off behind the restrooms, and before I can even think, he spins me around, grabs my hands, and places them on the wall.

"Don't move." I suck in a breath as I feel him lift my skirt and slide straight back into me. I keep my hands where they are as he moves behind me, fucking me like I wanted. He always knows exactly what to do without me having to ask. "Hands," he whispers.

I put them back on the wall, and he chuckles at my huff of annoyance.

"They went behind there."

I come as I hear those words.

It didn't take me long.

I'm already worked up, and his cock always hits that perfect spot, no matter what angle. He knows how to please me.

"Gotta go, love. We can finish this in the car." He pulls my skirt down, grabs my hand, and then we're running again. I can't help the giggle that escapes. And all I see is his smiling face as he looks back at me.

He takes me to the car.

Fucks me some more.

Then at home, he eats me for dessert.

And I wonder…

Is it him who has the pregnancy sex craving, or am I just that damn lucky?

THIRTY-ONE

Kyson
_____

ONE YEAR LATER...

"Nope, no. Not happening," I hear Kenzo say on the phone.

"Kenzo, she's sick. Help her."

"No, she has green shit in her nose. I am *not* touching that." Kalilah grabs the phone from my hand, and I can tell she's mad.

"Kenzo Hunter, if you can kill someone, you can wipe your niece's nose. Now *do it*."

"Fuck, you're bossy." He has us on FaceTime, so we watch as he puts the phone down and crawls over our daughter, who is a bundle of joy and always seems to stop crying when Kenzo holds her.

And it took some time to even get him to hold her.

He got sick of hearing her cry every time he came over. First it was because she wasn't latching correctly to Kalilah's boobs, then it was gas. It's been never-ending shit, but the best kind of never-ending shit, especially when she is happy.

Well, those are my favorite days.

Today, Kalilah had a doctor's appointment, and she asked that I take her, so I asked Kenzo to babysit.

He agreed as long as she was asleep.

She was.

But not for long.

Lyla has been an amazing baby at night and sleeps all the way through. But during the day is another story.

And Lyla really likes Kenzo.

Kalilah moved back in with me about a month later. She tried to stand her ground, but she missed my house too much and preferred to sleep next to me. Her old room is now Lyla's room, and my spare room is where her parents stay when they come to visit. They have come almost every month and are even talking about moving here. They met my brothers, and surprisingly, they loved them. Zuko even had a full conversation with her father. Go figure!

Her father told me before he left that he's glad she is surrounded by such good men.

Little does he know...

"Stop moving and hold still." We both look at Kenzo on the screen. "You are such a gremlin, you know that, right? You need to learn to wipe your own damn nose."

"Kenzo, she isn't even six months old. She can't even crawl," I remind him.

"Yeah, shut up. She's more clever than she looks. She's already getting men to do her dirty work."

Lyla giggles, and we watch as he leans down to pick her up. Her little arms wrap around his throat, and she lays her head there.

He doesn't move to pick up the phone.

Kenzo has told us he never wants kids—that she is more than enough for him. And I believe him. I was never sure if I wanted a family. Honestly, I never believed it would happen with who we are, but it has. And I have the best fucking woman to have this lifestyle with.

Kalilah stopped working when she was around seven months pregnant. Her morning sickness came back in the last trimester, so it was best she quit. They did tell her she was welcome back any time, which made her extremely happy.

"We'll be home later." I hang up. We know she will be fine with him. He only FaceTimes us when he doesn't know what to do.

"Kalilah."

"Hmm…" she says from the passenger seat. Her eyes are on her phone as she looks at the photographs she took of Lyla this morning.

"I still want to marry you," I tell her.

She lifts her head and turns it toward me. "I don't know if I want that," she replies quietly.

I pull the car over and face her. "It's okay, I can wait."

She bites her lip. "What if I never want it?"

"Then I will wait forever. One day you will say yes. It's only a matter of time. And I'm in no rush. Maybe I'll knock you up again, and we can create our own elite team."

"Our kids will not be trained killers," she warns, pointing a finger at me.

I laugh at her seriousness.

"I am deadly serious," she insists.

Placing a finger under her chin, I lift it and kiss

her on the lips. I'll never get sick of it, of her, or how she tastes.

She was amazing when she gave birth. I didn't think I could love anyone as much as I love her, but how wrong I was. I love both my girls so much more.

What a powerful woman she is.

"And I don't want any more kids. That would be madness," she informs me, looking into my eyes. I see her smirk at the use of our safe word. "But I am always happy to keep on trying for kids."

"I like the sound of that." I kiss her again just as the phone rings, and Kenzo's face appears on the screen.

"She peed on me. You better be on your way, or I'm leaving her." He hangs up, and we both laugh. He said the exact same thing last time, and we got home to find them both asleep on the floor next to each other.

"You don't think he would actually leave her, do you?" Kalilah asks. "I mean, it's not like we ask him a lot to help, and last time he said the same thing."

"It's empty threats. He hates that he's already wrapped around her finger and can't explain why." She nods because she knows it's true. Lyla cries, and Kenzo reaches for her without even asking.

"Do you think he will have kids?" she asks.

"Nope, not a chance in hell." I laugh.

"They may have said the same about you, and look at you now," she points out, and I brush it off.

"Kenzo doesn't date. Never has. I don't even think he's fucked the same woman more than once. Maybe a girl from the red room, but even then, he goes to cut, not to fuck."

I reach for Kalilah, sliding my hand between her legs. "Want a quickie before we get back? I bet I can make you come in two minutes." She bites her lip and undoes her seat belt.

I pull the car over, and she climbs over onto my lap.

"Make it one minute, and we have a deal." She chuckles as she frees my cock.

"Deal," I say, and I do exactly that, making her scream.

And she thanks God.

When really, she should be thanking my cock.

He's a masterpiece.

Also by T.L. SMITH

Black (Black #1)

Red (Black #2)

White (Black #3)

Green (Black #4)

Kandiland

Pure Punishment (Standalone)

Antagonize Me (Standalone)

Degrade (Flawed #1)

Twisted (Flawed #2)

Distrust (Smirnov Bratva #1) FREE

Disbelief (Smirnov Bratva #2)

Defiance (Smirnov Bratva #3)

Dismissed (Smirnov Bratva #4)

Lovesick (Standalone)

Lotus (Standalone)

Savage Collision (A Savage Love Duet book 1)

Savage Reckoning (A Savage Love Duet book 2)

Buried in Lies

Distorted Love (Dark Intentions Duet 1)

Sinister Love (Dark Intentions Duet 2)

Cavalier (Crimson Elite #1)

Anguished (Crimson Elite #2)

Conceited (Crimson Elite #3)

Insolent (Crimson Elite #4)

Playette

Love Drunk

Hate Sober

Heartbreak Me (Duet #1)

Heartbreak You (Duet #2)

My Beautiful Poison

My Wicked Heart

My Cruel Lover

Chained Hands

Locked Hearts

Sinful Hands

Shackled Hearts

Reckless Hands

Arranged Hearts

Unlikely Queen

A Villain's Kiss

A Villain's Lies

Connect with T.L Smith by tlsmithauthor.com

About the Author

USA Today Best Selling Author T.L. Smith loves to write her characters with flaws so beautiful and dark you can't turn away. Her books have been translated into several languages. If you don't catch up with her in her home state of Queensland, Australia you can usually find her travelling the world, either sitting on a beach in Bali or exploring Alcatraz in San Francisco or walking the streets of New York.

Connect with me tlsmithauthor.com

Printed in Great Britain
by Amazon